EXPECTING
THE EARL'S BABY

EXPECTING
THE EARL'S BABY

BY

JESSICA GILMORE

MILLS & BOON

First published in Great Britain 2015
by Mills & Boon, an imprint of Harlequin (UK) Limited,
Large Print edition 2015
Eton House, 18-24 Paradise Road,
Richmond, Surrey, TW9 1SR

© 2015 Jessica Gilmore

ISBN: 978-0-263-25667-3

Harlequin (UK) Limited's policy is to use papers that
are natural, renewable and recyclable products and made
from wood grown in sustainable forests. The logging
and manufacturing processes conform to the legal
environmental regulations of the country of origin.

Printed and bound in Great Britain
by CPI Antony Rowe, Chippenham, Wiltshire

For Carla
A book about sisters, for my sister
Love Jessica x

PROLOGUE

'OH, NO!'

Daisy Huntingdon-Cross skidded to a halt on the icy surface and regarded her car with dismay.

No, dismay was for a dropped coffee or spilling red wine on a white T-shirt. Her chest began to thump as panic escalated. *This*, Daisy thought as she stared at the wall of snow surrounding her suddenly flimsy-seeming tyres, *this* was a catastrophe.

The snow, which had fallen all afternoon and evening, might have made a picturesque background for the wedding photos she had spent the past twelve hours taking, but it had begun to drift—and right now it was packed in tightly around her tyres. Her lovely, bright, quirky little city car, perfect for zooming around London in, was, she was rapidly realising, horribly vulnerable in heavy snow and icy conditions.

Daisy carefully shifted her heavy bag to her

other shoulder and looked around. It was the only car in the car park.

In fact, she was the only person in the car park. No, scratch that, she was possibly the only person in the whole castle. A shiver ran down her spine, not entirely as a result of the increasing cold and the snow seeping through her very inadequate brogues. Hawksley Castle was a wonderfully romantic venue in daylight and when it was lit up at night. But when you were standing underneath the parapets, the great tower a craggy, shadowy silhouette looming above you and the only light a tepid glow from the lamp at the edge of the car park it wasn't so much romantic, more the setting for every horror film she had ever seen.

'Just don't go running into the woods.' She cast a nervous glance over her shoulder. The whole situation was bad enough without introducing the supernatural into it.

Besides it was Valentine's Day. Surely the only ghosts abroad today had to be those of lovers past?

Daisy shivered again as her feet made the painful transition from wet and cold to freezing. She stamped them with as much vigour as she could muster as she thought furiously.

Why had she stayed behind to photograph the

departing guests, all happily packed into mini-buses at the castle gates and whisked off to the local village where hot toddies and roaring fires awaited them? She could have left three hours ago, after the first dance and long before the snow had changed from soft flakes to a whirling mass of icy white.

But, no, she always had to take it that step further, offer that bit more than her competitors—including the blog, complete with several photographs, that she'd promised would be ready to view by midnight.

Midnight wasn't that far away…

'Okay.' Her voice sounded very small in the empty darkness but talking aloud gave her a sense of normality. 'One, I can go into the village. It's only a couple of miles.' Surely the walking would warm up her feet? 'Two, I can try and scoop the worst of the snow off…' She cast a doubtful glance at the rest of the car park. The ever heavier snowfall had obliterated her footprints; it was like standing on a thick, very cold white carpet. An ankle-deep carpet. 'Three…' She was out of options. Walk or scoop, that was it.

'Three—I get you some snow chains.'

Daisy didn't quite manage to stifle a small

screech as deep masculine tones broke in on her soliloquy. She turned, almost losing her footing in her haste, and skidded straight into a fleece-clad chest.

It was firm, warm, broad. Not a ghost. Probably not a werewolf. Or a vampire. Supernatural creatures didn't wear fleece as far as she knew.

'Where did you come from? You frightened the life out of me.' Daisy stepped back, scowling at her would-be rescuer. At least she hoped he was a rescuer.

'I was just locking up. I thought all the wedding guests were long gone.' His gaze swept over her. 'You're hardly dressed for this weather.'

'I was dressed for a wedding.' She tugged the hem of her silk dress down. 'I'm not a guest though, I'm the photographer.'

'Right.' His mouth quirked into a half smile. The gesture changed his rather severe face into something much warmer. Something much more attractive. He was tall—taller than Daisy who, at nearly six feet, was used to topping most men of her acquaintance—with scruffy dark hair falling over his face.

'Photographer or guest you probably don't want to be hanging around here all night so I'll get some chains and we'll try and get this tin can of yours on the road. You really should put on some winter tyres.'

'It's not a tin can and there's very little call for winter tyres in London.'

'You're not in London,' he pointed out silkily.

Daisy bit her lip. He had a point and she wasn't really in any position to argue. 'Thank you.'

'No worries, wouldn't want you to freeze to death on the premises. Think of the paperwork. Talking of which, you're shivering. Come inside and warm up. I can lend you some socks and a coat. You can't drive home like that.'

Daisy opened her mouth to refuse and then closed it again. He didn't seem like an axe murderer and she was getting more and more chilled by the second. If it was a choice between freezing to death and taking her chances inside she was definitely veering towards the latter. Besides… 'What time is it?'

'About eleven, why?'

She'd never get home in time to post the blog. 'I don't suppose…' She tried her most winning smile, her cheeks aching with the cold. 'I don't suppose I can borrow your Wi-Fi first? There's something I really need to do.'

'At this time of night?'

'It's part of my job. It won't take long.' Daisy gazed up at him hoping her eyes portrayed beseeching and hopeful with a hint of professionalism, not freezing cold and pathetic. Their eyes snagged and the breath hitched in her throat.

'I suppose you can use it while you warm up.' The smile was still playing around his mouth and Daisy's blood began to heat at the expression in his eyes. If he turned it up a little more she wouldn't need a jumper and socks, her own internal system would have defrosted her quite nicely.

He held out a hand. 'Seb, I look after this place.'

Daisy took the outstretched hand, her heart skipping a beat as their fingers touched. 'I'm Daisy. Nice to meet you, Seb.'

He didn't answer, reaching out and taking her bag, shouldering it with ease as he turned and began to tread gracefully through the ever thickening snow.

'"Mark my footsteps, my good page,"' Daisy sang under her breath as she took advantage of the pressed-down snow and hopped from one imprint to the other. Tall, dark, handsome and coming to her rescue on Valentine's Day? It was almost too good to be true.

CHAPTER ONE

Six weeks later...

DÉJÀ-VU RIPPLED DOWN Daisy's spine as she rounded the path. It was all so familiar and yet so different.

The last time she had been at Hawksley the castle and grounds had been covered in snow, a fantasy winter wonderland straight out of a historical film. Today the courtyard lawn was the pale green of spring, crocuses and primroses peeking out at the unseasonably warm sun. The old Norman keep rose majestically on her left, the thick grey stone buttresses looking much as they must have looked nearly one thousand years ago, a stark contrast to ye olde charm of the three-storey Tudor home attached to it at right angles.

And straight ahead of her the Georgian house.

Daisy swallowed, every instinct screaming at her to turn and run. She could wait a few weeks, try again then. Maybe try a letter instead. After all, it was still such early days...

But no. She straightened her shoulders. That was the coward's way out and she had been raised better than that. Confront your problems head-on, that was what her father always told her.

Besides, she really needed to talk to somebody. She didn't want to face her family, not yet, and none of her friends would understand. He was the only person who this affected in the same way.

Or not. But she had to take the risk.

Decision made, smile plastered on and she was ready to go. If she could just find him that was…

The castle had a very closed-off air. The small ticket office was shut, a sign proclaiming that the grounds and keep wouldn't be open until Whitsun. Daisy swivelled trying to find signs of life.

Nobody.

There was a small grey door set at the end of the Georgian wing, which she recognised from her earlier visit. It was as good a place to start as any.

Daisy walked over, taking her time and breathing in the fresh spring air, the warm sun on her back giving her courage as she pushed at the door.

'Great.' It was firmly locked and there was no bell, 'You'd think they didn't want visitors,' she muttered. Well, want them or not she was here. Daisy knocked as hard as she could, her knuckles smarting at the impact, then stood back and waited, anticipation twisting her stomach.

The door swung open. Slowly. Daisy inhaled and held her breath. Would he remember her?

Would he believe her?

A figure appeared at the door. She exhaled, torn between disappointment and a secret shameful relief. Unless Seb had aged twenty-five years, lost six inches and changed gender this wasn't him.

Daisy pushed her trilby hat further back and gave the stern-looking woman guarding the door marked 'private' an appealing smile. 'Excuse me, can you tell me where I can find Seb?'

Her appeal was met with crossed arms and a gorgonish expression. 'Seb?' There was an incredulous tone to her voice.

The message was loud and clear; smiling wasn't going to cut it. On the other hand she hadn't been instantly turned to stone so it wasn't a total loss.

'Yes.' Daisy bit her lip in a sudden panic. She had got his name right, hadn't she? So much of that night was a blur…

'The handyman,' she added helpfully. *That* she remembered.

'We have an estate maintenance crew.' The gorgon sniffed. Actually *sniffed*. 'But none of them

are named Seb. Maybe you have the wrong place?'
She looked Daisy up and down in a manner that
confirmed that, in her eyes, Daisy most definitely
did have the wrong place.

Maybe it was the lipstick? Real Real Red wasn't
a shade everyone liked. It was so very red after
all but it usually made Daisy feel ready for anything. Even today.

It was like being back at school under her head-
mistress's disappointed eye. Daisy resisted the
urge to tug her tailored shorts down to regulation
knee length and to button up the vintage waistcoat
she had thrown on over her white T-shirt.

She took a step back and straightened her shoulders, ready for war. She had replayed this morning over and over in her mind. At no point had
she anticipated not actually seeing Seb. Or finding out he didn't exist.

What if he was a ghost after all?

Surely not. Daisy wasn't entirely certain what
ectoplasm actually was but she was pretty sure
it was cold and sticky. Ghosts weren't made of
warm, solid muscle.

No, no dwelling on the muscles. Or the warmth.
She pushed the thought out of her mind as firmly

as she could and adopted her best, haughty public schoolgirl voice. 'This is Hawksley Castle, isn't it?'

Of course it was. Nowhere else had the utterly unique blend of Norman keep, Tudor mansion and Georgian country home that ensured Hawksley remained top of the country's best-loved stately homes list—according to *Debutante* magazine anyway.

But Daisy wasn't interested in the historical significance of the perfectly preserved buildings. She simply wanted to gain access to the final third of the castle, the Georgian wing marked 'private'.

'Yes, this is Hawksley Castle and we are not open until Whitsun. So, I suggest, miss, that you return and purchase a ticket then.'

'Look.' Daisy was done with playing nice. 'I'm not here to sightsee. I was here six weeks ago for the Porter-Halstead wedding and got snowed in. Seb helped me and I need to see him. To say thank you,' she finished a little lamely but there was no way she was telling this woman her real motivation for visiting. She'd be turned to stone for sure.

The gorgon raised an eyebrow. 'Six weeks later?'

'I'm not here for a lesson in manners.' Daisy regretted the snap the second it left her mouth. 'I've been…busy. But better late than never. I thought he was the handyman. He certainly—' seemed good with his hands flashed through her mind and she coloured '—seemed to know his way around.' Oh, yes, that he did.

Nope. No better.

'But he definitely works here. He has an office. Tall, dark hair?' Melting dark green eyes, cheekbones she could have cut herself on and a firm mouth. A mouth he really knew how to use.

Daisy pulled her mind firmly back to the here and now. 'He had a shovel and snow chains, that's why I thought he was the handyman but maybe he's the estate manager?'

Unless he had been a wedding guest putting on a very good act? Had she made a terrible mistake? No, he hadn't been dressed like a wedding guest, had known his way around the confusing maze behind the baize door in the Georgian wing.

She was going to have to get tough. 'Listen,' she began then stopped as something wet and cold snuffled its way into her hand. Looking down, she saw a pair of mournful brown eyes gazing up at her. 'Monty!'

Proof! Proof that she wasn't going crazy and proof that Seb was here.

Crouching down to scratch behind the springer spaniel's floppy brown ears, Daisy broke into a croon. 'How are you, handsome boy? It's lovely to see you again. Now if you could just persuade this lady here that I need to see your master that will be brilliant.' She couldn't help throwing a triumphant glance over at her adversary.

'Monty! Here, boy! Monty! Here I say.' Peremptory tones rang across the courtyard and Daisy's heart began to speed up, blood rushing around her body in a giddying carousel. Slowly she got back up, leaving one hand on the spaniel's head, more for strength and warmth, and half turned, a smile on her face.

'Hi, Seb.'

It had been a long morning. It wasn't that Seb wasn't grateful for his expensive education, his academic credentials and his various doctorates but there were times when he wondered just what use being able to recite Latin verse and debate the use of cavalry at Thermopylae was.

Business studies, basic accountancy, and how to repair, heat and conserve an ancient money pit without whoring her out like a restoration actress would have been far more useful.

He needed a business plan. Dipping into what was left of the estate's capital would only get him so far. Somehow the castle needed to pay for itself—and soon.

And now his dog was being disobedient, making eyes at a blonde woman improbably dressed in shorts and a trilby hat teamed with a garish waistcoat. Shorts. In *March*. On the other hand… Seb's eyes raked the slender, long legs appreciably; his dog had good taste.

'Monty! I said here. I am so sorry…' His voice trailed off as the woman straightened and turned. Seb felt his breath whoosh out as he clocked the long blonde hair, blue eyes, tilted nose and a mouth that had haunted him for the last six weeks. 'Daisy?'

'Hello, Seb. You never call, you don't write.' An undercurrent of laughter lilted through her voice and he had to firm his mouth to stop a responsive smile creeping out. What on earth had brought the wedding photographer back to his door? For a few days afterwards he had wondered if she might get in touch. And what he would say if she did.

For six weeks afterwards he had considered getting in touch himself.

'Neither did you.'

'No.' Her eyelashes fluttered down and she looked oddly vulnerable despite the ridiculous hat tilted at a rakish angle and the bright lipstick. 'Seb, could we talk?'

She sounded serious and Seb tensed, his hands curling into apprehensive fists. 'Of course, come on in.' He gestured for her to precede him through the door. 'Thanks, Mrs Suffolk, I'll take it from here.' He smiled at his most faithful volunteer and she moved aside with a sniff of clear disapproval.

'I don't think she likes me,' Daisy whispered.

'She doesn't like anyone. Anyone under thirty and female anyway.' He thought about the statement. 'Actually anyone under thirty *or* any female.'

Seb led the way through the narrow hallway, Monty at his heels. The courtyard entrance led directly into what had once been the servants' quarters, a warren of windy passageways, small rooms and back staircases designed to ensure the maids and footmen of long ago could go about their duties without intruding on the notice of the family they served.

Now it held the offices and workrooms necessary for running the vast estate. The few staff that lived in had cottages outside the castle walls and

Seb slept alone in a castle that had once housed dozens.

It would make sense to convert a floor of unused bedrooms and offer overnight hospitality to those who booked the Tudor Hall for weddings rather than chucking them out into the nearby hotels and guest houses. But it wasn't just the expense that put him off. It was one thing having tourists wandering around the majestic keep, one thing to rent out the spectacular if dusty, chilly and impractical hall. The Georgian wing was his home. Huge, ancient, filled with antiques, ghosts and dusty corners. *Home.*

And walking beside him was the last person to have stayed there with him.

'Welcome back.' Seb noted how, despite her general air of insouciance, she was twisting her hands together nervously. 'Nice hat.'

'Thanks.' She lifted one hand and touched it self-consciously. 'Every outfit needs a hat.'

'I don't recall you wearing one last time.'

'I was dressed for work then.'

The words hung heavily in the air and Seb was instantly transported back. Back to the slide of a zip, the way her silky dress had slithered to the ground in one perfect movement.

Definitely no hat on that occasion, just glittering pins in her hair. It was a shame. He would have quite liked to have seen her wearing it when she had lain on his sofa, golden in the candlelight, eyes flushed from the champagne. Champagne and excitement. The hat and nothing else.

He inhaled, long and deep, trying to ignore the thrumming of his heart, the visceral desire the memory evoked.

Seb stopped and reconsidered his steps. The old estate office was an incongruous mix of antique desk, sofa and rug mixed with metal filing cabinets and shelves full of things no one wanted to throw away but didn't know what else to do with.

Now, with Daisy's reappearance, it was a room with ghosts of its own. Six-week-old ghosts with silken skin, low moans and soft, urgent cries. Taking her back there would be a mistake.

Instead he opened the discreet doors that led into the front of the house. 'Let's go to the library.' It wasn't cowardice that had made him reconsider. It was common sense. His mouth quirked at the corner. 'As you can probably tell, the house hasn't received the memo for the warmest spring in ten years and it takes several months for the chill to dissipate. The library is the warmest room in the whole place—probably because it's completely non-modernised. The velvet drapes may be dusty and dark but they keep the cold out.'

Daisy adjusted her hat again, her hands still nervous. 'Fine.'

He pushed the heavy wooden door open, standing aside to let her go in first. 'So, this is quite a surprise.'

She flushed, the colour high on her cheekbones. 'A nice one, I hope.' But she didn't meet his eye. He stilled, watching her. Something was going on, something way beyond a desire for his company.

Daisy walked into the oak-panelled room and stood, looking curiously about her. Seb leant against the door for a moment, seeing the room through her eyes; did she find it shabby? Intimidating? It was an odd mixture of both. The overflowing floor-to-ceiling bookshelves covered two of the walls; the dark oak panelling was hung with gloomy family portraits and hunting scenes. Even the fireplace was large enough to roast at least half an ox, the imposing grate flanked by a massive marble lintel. All that the library needed was an irascible old man to occupy one of the wingback chairs and Little Lord Fauntleroy to come tripping in.

She wandered over to one of the shelves and pulled out a book, dust flying into the air. 'Good to see the owner's a keen reader.'

'Most of the English books have been read. That's the Latin section.'

She tilted her chin. 'Latin or not, they still need dusting.'

'I'll get the footmen right on it. Sit down.' He gestured to a chair. 'Would you like a drink?'

'Will a footman bring it?'

'No.' He allowed himself a smile. 'There's a kettle in that corner. It's a long way from here to the kitchen.'

'Practical. Tea, please. Do you have Earl Grey?'

'Lemon or milk?'

Seating herself gingerly in one of the velvet chairs, the dusty book still in her hand, she raised an elegantly arched eyebrow. 'Lemon? How civilised. Could I just have hot water and lemon, please?'

'Of course.'

It only took a minute to make the drinks but the time out was needed. It was unsettling, having her here in his private space, the light floral scent of her, the long legs, the red, red lipstick drawing attention to her wide, full mouth. The problem with burying yourself with work twenty-four-seven, Seb reflected as he sliced the lemon, was that it left you ill prepared for any human interaction. Especially the feminine kind.

Which was rather the point.

'A proper cup and saucer. You have been well brought up.' She held up the delicately patterned porcelain as he handed it to her and examined it. 'Wedgwood?'

'Probably.'

Seb seated himself opposite, as if about to interview her, and sat back, doing his best to look as if he were at his ease, as if her unexpected reappearance hadn't totally thrown him. 'How's peddling ridiculous dreams and overblown fantasies going?'

Daisy took a sip of her drink, wincing at the heat. 'Business is good, thanks. Busy.'

'I'm not surprised.' He eyed her critically. 'Engagement shoots, fifteen-hour days, blogs. When you work out your hourly rate you're probably barely making minimum wage.' Not that he was one to talk.

'It's expected.' Her tone was defensive. 'Anyone can get a mate to point a camera nowadays. Wedding photographers need to provide more, to look into the soul of the couple. To make sure there isn't one second of their special day left undocumented.'

Seb shook his head. 'Weddings! What happened to simple and heartfelt? Not that I'm complaining. We are already booked up for the next two years. It's crazy. So much money on just one day.'

'But it's the happiest day of their lives.'

'I sincerely hope not. It's just the first day, not the marriage,' he corrected her. 'Romantic fantasies like that are the biggest disservice to marriage. People pour all their energy and money into just one day—they should be thinking about their lives together. Planning that.'

'You make it sound so businesslike.'

'It *is* businesslike,' he corrected her. 'Marriage is like anything else. It's only successful if the participants share goals. Know exactly what they are signing up for. Mark my words, a couple who go into marriage with a small ceremony and a robust life plan will last a lot longer than fools who get into debt with one over-the-top day.'

'No, you're wrong.' Daisy leant forward, her eyes lit up. 'Two people finding each other, plighting their troth in front of all their friends and family, what could be more romantic than that?' Her voice trailed off, the blue eyes wistful.

Seb tried not to let his mouth quirk into a smile but the temptation was too much. 'Did you just say plight your troth? Is that what you write in your blogs?'

'My couples say my blogs are one of the most romantic parts of their special day.' Her colour was high. 'That's why I do the engagement shoots, to get to know each couple individually, know what makes them tick. And no.' She glared at him. 'Even with the extras I still make well over the minimum wage and no one ever complains. In fact, one couple have just asked me to come back to document their pregnancy and take the first photographs of their baby.'

'Of course they did.' He couldn't keep the sarcasm out of his voice. 'The only thing guaranteed to waste more money than a wedding is a baby.'

Her already creamy skin paled, her lips nearly blue. 'Then you probably don't want to hear that you're going to be a father. I'm pregnant, Seb. That's what I came here to say.'

As soon as she blurted the words out she regretted it. It wasn't how she'd planned to tell him; her carefully prepared lead up to the announcement abandoned in the heat of the moment. At least she had shaken him out of the cool complacency; Seb had shot upright, the green eyes hard, his mouth set firm.

'Are you sure?'

Oh, yes. She was sure. Two tests a day for the past week sure. 'I have a test in my bag, I can take it here and now if you like.' It wasn't the kind of thing she'd usually offer to an almost stranger but the whole situation was embarrassing enough, another step into mortification alley wouldn't hurt.

'No, that won't be necessary.' He ran a hand through his hair. 'But we used… I mean, we were careful.'

It was almost funny—almost—that she and this man opposite could have spent a night being as intimate as two people could be. Had explored and tasted and touched. Had teased and caressed and been utterly uninhibited. And yet they didn't know each other at all. He couldn't even use the word 'condom' in front of her.

'We did.' Daisy summoned up all her poise and looked at him as coolly and directly as she could manage, trying to breathe her panicked pulse into submission, to still the telltale tremor in her hands. 'At least, we did the first and second time. I'm not sure we were thinking clearly after that.'

Not that they had been thinking clearly at all. Obviously. It was easy to blame the snowfall, the intimacy of being alone in the fairy-tale landscape, the champagne. That he had come to her rescue. But it still didn't add up. It had been the most incredible, the most intense and the most out-of-character night of Daisy's life.

A muscle was beating along the stubbled jawline; his eyes were still hard, unreadable. 'How do you know it's mine?'

She had been prepared for this question, it was totally reasonable for him to ask and yet a sharp stab of disappointment hit her. 'It has to be yours.' She lifted her chin and eyed him defiantly. 'There is no one else, there hasn't been, not for a long time. I usually only do long-term relationships and I split up from my last boyfriend nine months ago.' She needed to make him understand. 'That night, it wasn't usual. It wasn't how I normally behave.'

'Right.'

'You can check, have a test. Only not until after it's born. It's safer that way.'

His eyes locked onto hers. 'You're keeping it, then?'

Another reasonable question and yet one she hadn't even thought to ask herself. 'Yes. Look, Seb, you don't have to decide anything right now. I'm not here for answers or with demands. I just thought you should know but...'

'Hold on.' He stood up with a lithe grace, hand held out to cut her off. 'I need to think. Don't go anywhere, can you promise me that? I won't be long, I just, I just need some air. Come on, Monty.'

'Wait!' It was too late, he had whirled out of the door, the spaniel close to his heels. Daisy had half got up but sank back down into the deep-backed chair as the heavy oak door closed with a thud.

'That went better than I expected,' she murmured. She was still here and, okay, he hadn't fallen to his knees and pledged to love the baby for ever but neither had she been turned out barefoot onto his doorstep.

And wasn't his reaction more natural? Questioning disbelief? Maybe that should have been hers as well. Daisy slid her hand over her midriff, marvelling at the flat tautness, no visible clue that anything had changed. And yet she hadn't been shocked or upset or considered for even a nano-second that she wouldn't have the baby.

Its conception might be an accident in most people's eyes but not in Daisy's. It was something else entirely. It was a miracle.

One hour later, more hot lemon and three pages of a beautiful old hardback edition of *Pride and Prejudice* read over and over again, Daisy admitted defeat. Wait, he had said. How long did he mean? She hadn't promised him anyway; he had disappeared before she could form the words.

But she couldn't leave without making sure he had a way of getting in touch. She hadn't thought last time, hadn't slipped her card into his hand or pocket with a smile and invitation. Had part of her hoped he would track her down anyway? Perform a modern-day quest in pursuit of her love. The hopeless romantic in her had. The hopeless romantic never learned.

But this wasn't about challenges. It was more important than that. Rummaging in her bag, Daisy pulled out one of her business cards. Stylish, swirling script and a daisy motif proclaimed 'Daisy Photos. Weddings, portraits and lifestyle.' Her number, website and Twitter handle listed clearly below. She paused for a second and then laid the card on the tea tray with a hand that only trembled a little. It was up to him now.

She closed her eyes for a moment, allowing her shoulders to sag under the weight of her disappointment. She had been prepared for anger, denial. Naively, she had hoped he might be a little excited. She hadn't expected him to just *leave*.

Her car was where she'd left it, parked at a slant just outside the imposing gates. If she had swallowed her pride and accepted the Range Rover her father had offered her then she wouldn't have been snowed in all those weeks ago.

Daisy shook her head trying to dislodge unwanted tears prickling the backs of her eyes. It had all seemed so perfect, like a scene from one of her favourite romantic comedies. When it was clear that she was stuck, Seb had ransacked the leftovers from the wedding buffet, bringing her a picnic of canapés and champagne. And she had curled up on the shabby sofa in his office as they talked and drank, and somehow she had found herself confiding in him, trusting him. Kissing him.

She raised her hands to her lips, remembering how soft his kiss had been. At first anyway…

Right. Standing here reliving kisses wasn't going to change anything. Daisy unlocked her car, and took one last long look at the old castle keep, the grim battlements softened by the amber spring sun.

'Daisy!'

She paused for a moment and inhaled long and deep before swivelling round, trying to look as unconcerned as possible, and leaning back against her car.

Her heart began to thump. Loudly.

He wasn't her type at all. Her type was clean-shaven, their eyes didn't hold a sardonic gleam under quizzical eyebrows and look as if they were either laughing at you or criticising you. Her usual type didn't wear their dark hair an inch too long and completely unstyled and walk around in old mud-splattered jeans, although she had to admit they were worn in all the right places.

And Daisy Huntingdon-Cross had never as much as had a coffee with a man in a logoed fleece. The black garment might bear the Hawksley Castle crest but it was still a fleece.

So why had her pulse sped up, heat pooling in the pit of her stomach? Daisy allowed the car to take more of her weight, grateful for its support.

'Come back inside, we haven't finished talking yet.' It wasn't a request.

The heat melted away, replaced by a growing indignation. Daisy straightened up, folding her arms. 'We haven't *started* talking. I gave you an hour.'

'I know.' She had been hoping for penitent but he was totally matter-of-fact. 'I think better outside.'

'And?' Daisy wanted to grab the word back the second she uttered it. It sounded as if she had been on tenterhooks waiting for him to proclaim her fate. The kernel of truth in that thought made her squirm.

He ran a hand through his hair. The gesture was unexpectedly boyish and uncertain. 'This would be easier if we just went back inside.'

She raised her eyebrows. 'You think better outside.'

He smiled at that, his whole expression lightening. It changed him completely, the eyes softer, the slightly harsh expression warmer.

'Yes. But do you?'

'Me?'

'I have a proposition for you and you need to be thinking clearly. Are you?'

No. No, she wasn't. Daisy wasn't sure she'd had a clear thought since she had accepted that first glass of champagne, had hotly defended her livelihood as her rescuer had quizzed and teased her and had found herself laughing, absurdly delighted as the stern expression had melted into something altogether different.

But she wasn't going to admit that. Not to him, barely to herself.

'Completely clearly.'

He looked sceptical but nodded. 'Then, Daisy, I think you should marry me.'

CHAPTER TWO

SEB DIDN'T EXACTLY expect Daisy to throw herself at his feet in gratitude, not really. And it would have made him uncomfortable if she had. But he was expecting that she would be touched by his proposal. Grateful even.

The incredulous laugh that bubbled out of that rather enchanting mouth was, therefore, a bit of a shock. Almost a blow—not to his heart, obviously, but, he realised with a painful jolt of self-awareness, to his ego. 'Are we in a regency novel? Seb, you haven't besmirched my honour. There's no need to do the honourable thing.'

The emphasis on the last phrase was scathing. And misplaced. There was every need. 'So why did you come here? I thought you wanted my help. Or are you after money? Is that it?'

Maybe the whole situation was some kind of clever entrapment. His hands curled into fists and he inhaled, long and deep, trying not to let the burgeoning anger show on his face.

'Of course not.' Her indignation was convincing and the tightness in his chest eased a little. 'I thought you should know first, that was all. I didn't come here for money or marriage or anything.'

'I see, you're planning to do this alone. And you want me to what? Pop over on a Sunday and take the baby to the park? Sleepovers once a month?' Seb could hear the scathing scorn punctuating each of his words and Daisy paled, taking a nervous step away, her hand fumbling for the car handle.

'I haven't really thought that far ahead.'

Seb took another deep breath, doing his best to sound reasonable as he grabbed the slight advantage. 'You work what? Fifteen hours a day at weekends? Not just weekends. People get married every day of the week now. What are you going to do for childcare?'

'I'll work something out.' The words were defiant but her eyes were troubled as she twisted her hand around the handle, her knuckles white with tension.

He put as much conviction into his voice as possible. 'You don't need to. Marry me.'

Her eyes were wide with confusion. 'Why? Why

on earth would you want to marry someone you barely know? Why would I agree to something so crazy?'

Seb gestured, a wide encompassing sweep of his arm taking in the lake, the woods and fields, the castle proudly overshadowing the landscape. 'Because that baby is my heir.'

Daisy stared at him. 'What?'

'The baby is my heir,' he repeated. 'Our baby. To Hawksley.'

'Don't be ridiculous. What has the castle got to do with the baby?'

'Not just the castle, the estate, the title, everything.'

'But—' she shook her head stubbornly '—you're the handyman, aren't you? You had a shovel and a fleece and that office.'

'The handyman?' He could see her point. If only his colleagues could see him now, it was all a long way from his quiet office tucked away in a corner of an Oxford college. 'In a way I guess I am— owner, handyman, manager, event-booker—running the estate is a hands-on job nowadays.'

'So that makes you what? A knight?'

'An earl. The Earl of Holgate.'

'An earl?' She laughed, slightly hysterically. 'Is

this some kind of joke? Is there a camera recording this?' She twisted around, checking the fields behind them.

'My parents died six months ago. I inherited the castle then.' The castle and a huge amount of debt but there was no need to mention that right away. She was skittish enough as it was.

'You're being serious?' He could see realisation dawning, the understanding in her widened eyes even as she stubbornly shook her head. 'Titles don't mean anything, not any more.'

'They do to me, to the estate. Look, Daisy, you came here because you knew it was the right thing to do. Well, marrying me is the right thing to do. That baby could be the next Earl of Holgate. You want to deny him that right? Illegitimate children are barred from inheriting.'

'The baby could be a girl.' She wasn't giving in easily.

'It doesn't matter, with the royal line of succession no longer male primogeniture there's every chance the rest of the aristocracy will fall into line.' He held his hand out, coaxing. 'Daisy, come back inside, let's talk about this sensibly.'

She didn't answer for a long moment and he could sense her quivering, desperate need to run.

He didn't move, just waited, hand held out towards her until she took a deep breath and nodded. 'I'll come inside. To talk about the baby. But I am not marrying you. I don't care whether you're an earl or a handyman. I don't know you.'

Seb took a deep breath, relief filling his lungs. All he needed was time. Time for her to hear him out, to give him a chance to convince her. 'Come on, then.'

Daisy pushed off the car and turned. Seb couldn't help taking a long appreciative look at her shapely rear as she bent slightly to relock the car. The tweed shorts fitted snugly, showing off her slender curves to perfection. He tore his eyes away, hurriedly focusing on the far hedge as she straightened and turned to join him, the blue eyes alight with curiosity.

'An earl,' she repeated. 'No wonder the gorgon was so reluctant to let me in.'

'Gorgon?' But he knew who she meant and his mouth quirked as she stared at him meaningfully. 'I don't think she's actually turned anyone to stone. Not yet. Mrs Suffolk's family have worked here for generations. She's a little protective.'

They reached the courtyard and Daisy started

to make for the back door where Mrs Suffolk still stood guard, protecting the castle against day trippers and other invaders. Seb slipped a hand through Daisy's arm, guiding her round the side of the house and onto the sweeping driveway with its vista down to the wooded valley below.

'Front door and a fresh start,' he said as they reached the first step. 'Hello, I'm Sebastian Beresford, Earl of Holgate.'

'Sebastian Beresford?' Her eyes narrowed. 'I know that name. You're not an earl, you're that historian.'

'I'm both. Even earls have careers nowadays.' Although how he was going to continue his academic responsibilities with running Hawksley was a problem he had yet to solve.

He held out his hand. 'Welcome to my home.'

Daisy stared at his hand for a moment before placing her cool hand in his. 'Daisy Huntingdon-Cross, it's a pleasure to meet you.'

Who? There it was, that faint elusive memory sharpened into focus. 'Huntingdon-Cross? Rick Cross and Sherry Huntingdon's daughter?'

No wonder she looked familiar! Rock royalty on their father's side and pure county on their mother's, the Huntingdon-Cross sisters were as renowned for their blonde, leggy beauty as they were infamous for their lifestyle. Each of them had been splashed across the tabloids at some point in their varied careers—and their parents were legends; rich, talented and famously in love.

Seb's heart began to pound, painfully thumping against his chest, the breath knocked from his lungs in one blow. This was not the plan, the quiet, businesslike, private union he intended.

This was *trouble*.

If he married this girl then the tabloids would have a field day. A Beresford and a Huntingdon-Cross would be front-page fodder to rival anything his parents had managed to stir up in their wake. All the work he had done to remain out of the press would be undone faster than he could say, 'I do.'

But if he didn't marry her then he would be disinheriting the baby. He didn't have any choice.

Seb froze as he took her hand, recognition dawning in his eyes.

'Huntingdon-Cross,' he repeated and Daisy dropped his hand, recoiling from the horror in his voice.

For a moment she contemplated pretending she

wasn't one of *those* Huntingdon-Crosses but a cousin, a far, far removed cousin. From the north. Of course, Seb didn't have to know that she didn't have any northern cousins.

But what was the point? He'd find out the truth soon enough and, besides, they might be wild and infuriating and infamous but they were hers. No matter how many titles or illustrious ancestors Seb had, he had no right to sneer at her family.

Daisy channelled her mother at her grandest, injecting as much froideur into her voice as she possibly could and tilting her chin haughtily. 'Yes. I'm the youngest. I believe the tabloids call me the former wild child if that helps.'

At this the green eyes softened and the corner of his mouth tilted; heat pooled in her stomach as her blood rushed in response. It was most unfair, the almost smile made him more human. More handsome.

More desirable.

'The one who got expelled from school?'

He had to bring that up. Daisy's face heated, the embarrassed flush spreading from her cheeks to her neck. He was an Oxford professor, he'd probably never met anyone who had been expelled before, let alone someone with barely an academic qualification to her name. 'I wasn't expelled exactly, they just asked me to leave.'

'Sounds like expulsion to me,' he murmured.

'It was ridiculously strict. It was almost impossible *not* to get expelled. Unless you were clever and studious like my sisters, that is.' Okay, it was eight years ago and Daisy had spent every minute of those eight years trying to prove her teachers wrong but it still rankled. Still hurt.

'The Mother Superior was always looking for a way to rid the school of the dullards like me. That way we didn't bring the exam average down.' She stared at him, daring him to react. He'd probably planned for the mother of his future children to have a batch of degrees to match his. His and her mortar boards.

'They expelled you for not being academic?'

'Well, not exactly. They expelled me for breaking bounds and going clubbing in London. But if I'd been predicted all As it would have been a slap on the wrist at the most. At least, probably,' she added, conscious she wasn't being entirely fair. 'There were pictures on the front page of *The Planet* and I think some of the parents were a little concerned.'

'A little?' Damn, the mouth was even more tilted now, the gleam intensifying in his eyes.

'I was sixteen. Most sixteen-year-old girls aren't locked away in stupid convent schools not even allowed to look at boys or wear anything but a hideous uniform. It isn't natural. But once front-page news, always front-page news. They hounded me for a bit until they realised how dull I really am. But I swear I could die at one hundred after a lifetime spent sewing smocks for orphaned lepers and my epitaph would read "Former wild child, Daisy, who was expelled from exclusive girls' school…"'

'Probably.' His voice was bleak again, the gleam gone as if it had never been there. 'Come on, let's go in. It's getting cold and one of us has unseasonably bare legs.'

Once the sun had started to set, the warmth quickly dissipated, the evening air tinted with a sharp breeze whipping around Daisy's legs. She shivered, the chill running up her arms and down her spine not entirely down to the cold. If she walked back into the castle everything would change.

But everything was changing anyway. Would it be easier if she didn't have to do this alone? It wasn't the proposal or the marriage of her dreams but maybe it was time to grow up. To accept that fairy tales were for children and that princes came in all shapes and sizes—as did earls.

Not that Seb's shape was an issue. She slid a glance over at him, allowing her eyes to run up his legs, the worn jeans clinging to his strong thighs and the slim hips, and up his torso, his lean muscled strength hidden by the shirt and fleece. But her body remembered the way he had picked her up without flinching, the play of his muscles under her hands.

No, his shape wasn't an issue.

But she had worked so hard to be independent. Not traded on her parents' names, not depended on their money. Would marrying for support, albeit emotional not financial, be any different from accepting it from her family?

At least she knew they loved her. A marriage without love wasn't to be considered. Not for her. She needed to make that clear so that they could move on and decide what was best for the baby.

'Where's the cook? The faithful retainers? The maids' bobbing curtsies?' Daisy expected that they would return to the library but instead Seb had led her through the baize doors and back through the tangle of passages to the kitchen. She would need a ball of thread to find her way back.

The whole house was a restoration project waiting to happen and the kitchen no exception but Daisy quite liked the old wooden cabinets, the ancient Aga and Monty slumped in front of it with his tail beating a steady rhythm on the flagstone floor. It didn't take much imagination to see the ghosts of small scullery maids, scuttling out into the adjoining utility room, an apple-cheeked cook rolling out pastry on the marbled worktops. Automatically she framed it, her mind selecting the right filter and the focal point of the shot.

Any of Daisy's friends would strip out the cabinets, install islands and breakfast bars and folding doors opening out into the courtyard—undoubtedly creating something stunning. And yet the kitchen would lose its heart, its distinctive soul.

Seb gestured to a low chair by the Aga. 'Do you want to sit there? It's the warmest spot in the room. No, there's no one else, just me. A cleaner comes in daily but I live alone.' He had opened a door that led to a pantry bigger than Daisy's entire kitchen. 'Are you vegetarian?'

'For a term in Year Eleven.'

'Good. Anything you…erm…really want to eat?' He sounded flustered and, as realisation dawned, her cheeks heated in tandem with his. It was going to be uncomfortable if neither of them could mention the pregnancy without embarrassment.

'Oh! You mean cravings? No, at least, not yet. But if I get a need for beetroot and coal risotto I'll make sure you're the first to know.'

The green eyes flashed. 'You do that.'

Daisy didn't want to admit it, even to herself, but she was tired. It had been a long week, excitement mixing with shock, happiness with worry and sleep had been elusive. It was soothing leaning back in the chair, the warmth from the Aga penetrating her bones. Monty rested his head on her feet as she watched Seb expertly chopping onions and grilling steaks.

'From the estate farm,' he said as he heated the oil. 'I'm pretty much self-sufficient, well, thanks to the tenant farmers I am.'

Neither of them mentioned the elephant in the room but the word was reverberating round and round her head. *Marriage.*

Was this what it would be like? Cosy evenings

in the kitchen? Rocking in a chair by the fire while Seb cooked. Maybe she should take up knitting.

'Did you mean what you said earlier, in the library? That marriage is a business?'

He didn't turn round but she saw his shoulders set rigid, the careless grace gone as he continued to sauté the vegetables.

'Absolutely. It's the only way it works.'

'Why?'

Seb stopped stirring and shot her a quick glance. 'What do you mean?'

Daisy was leaning back in the chair, her eyes half closed. His eyes flickered over her. The bright waistcoat, the hat and the lipstick were at odd with her pallor; she was pale, paler than he would have expected even at the end of a long, cold winter and the shadows under her eyes were a deep blue-grey. She looked exhausted. A primal protectiveness as unexpected as it was fierce rose up in him, almost overwhelming in its intensity. It wasn't what he wanted, the path he had chosen, but this was his responsibility; she was his responsibility.

She probably deserved better, deserved more than he could offer. But this was all he had.

'Why do you think that?'

Seb took a moment before answering, quickly

plating up the steaks and tipping the sautéed vegetables into a dish and putting it onto the table. He added a loaf of bread and a pat of butter and grabbed two steak knives and forks.

'Come and sit at the table,' he said. 'We can talk afterwards.'

It was like being on a first date. Worse, a blind date. A blind date where you suddenly lost all sense of speech, thought and taste. Was this his future? Sitting at a table with this woman, struggling for things to say?

'My grandparents ate every meal in the dining hall, even when it was just the two of them,' he said after a long, excruciating pause. 'Grandfather at the head of the table, grandmother at the foot. Even with the leaves taken out the table seats thirty.'

She put down her fork and stared at him. 'Could they hear each other?'

'They both had penetrating voices, although I don't know if they were natural or whether they developed them after fifty years of yelling at each other across fifteen foot of polished mahogany.' He half smiled, remembering their stubborn determination to keep to the ritual formality of their youth as the world changed around them.

'And what about your parents? Did they dispense with the rules and eat in here or did they like the distance?'

'Ah, my parents. It appears my parents spent most of their lives living wildly beyond their means. If I can't find a way to make Hawksley pay for itself within the next five years...' His voice trailed off. He couldn't articulate his worst fears: that he would be the Beresford who lost Hawksley Castle.

'Hence the handyman gig?'

'Hence the handyman gig. And the leave of absence from the university and hiring the hall out for weddings. It's a drop in the ocean but it's a start.'

'You need my sisters. Rose is in New York but she's a PR whizz and Violet is the most managing person I have ever met. I bet they could come up with a plan to save Hawksley.'

He needed more than a plan. He needed a miracle. 'My grandparents followed the rules all their lives. They looked after the estate, the people who lived on it. Lived up to their responsibilities. My parents were the opposite. They didn't spend much time here. Unless they were throwing a party. They preferred London, or the

Caribbean. Hawksley was a giant piggy bank, not a responsibility.'

Her eyes softened. 'What happened?'

'You must have read about them?' He pushed his half-empty plate away, suddenly sickened. 'If your parents are famous for their rock-solid marriage, mine were famous for their wildness—drugs, affairs, exotic holidays. They were always on the front pages. They divorced twice, remarried twice, each time in some ridiculous extravagant way. The first time they made me a pageboy. The second time I refused to attend.' He took a swig of water, his mouth dry.

It was awful, the resentment mixed with grief. When would it stop being so corrosive?

'Yes, now I remember. I'm so sorry. It was a plane crash, wasn't it?'

'They had been told it wasn't safe but the rules didn't apply to them. Or so they thought.'

Daisy pushed her seat back and stood up, collecting up the plates and waving away his offer of help. 'No, you cooked, I'll clear.'

He sat for a moment and watched as she competently piled the dishes and saucepans up by the side of the sink, rinsing the plates. He had to make it clear to her, make sure she knew exactly what he was offering. 'Marriage is a business.'

Daisy carried on rinsing, running hot water into the old ceramic sink. 'Once, perhaps…'

'I have to marry, have children, there are no other direct heirs and there's a danger the title will go extinct if I don't. But I don't want…' He squeezed his eyes shut for a brief moment, willing his pulse to stay calm. 'I won't have all the emotional craziness that comes with romantic expectations.'

She put the dishcloth down and turned, leaning against the sink as she regarded him. 'Seb, your parents, they weren't normal, you do know that? That level of drama isn't usual.'

He laughed. 'They were extreme, sure. But abnormal? They just didn't hide it the way the rest of the world does. I look at my friends, their parents. Sure, it's all hearts and flowers and nicknames at the beginning but I've lost count of how many relationships, how many marriages turn into resentment and betrayal and anger. No, maybe my ancestors knew what they were doing with a businesslike arrangement—compatibility, rules, peace.'

'My parents love each other even more than

they did when they got married.' A wistful smile curved Daisy's lips. 'Sometimes it's like it's just the two of them even when we're all there. They just look at each other and you can tell that at that moment it's like there's no one else in the room.'

'And how do you feel at those moments?'

Her eyelashes fluttered down. 'It can be a little lonely but…'

Exactly! Strengthened by her concession he carried on, his voice as persuasive as he could manage. 'Look, Daisy. There's no point me promising you romance because I don't believe in it. I can promise you respect, hopefully affection. I can promise that if we do this, become parents together, then I will love the baby and do my utmost to be the best parent I can.'

'I hope you will. But we don't need to be married to co-parent.'

'No,' he conceded.

'I've worked really hard to be my own person, build up my own business.' The blue eyes hardened. 'I don't depend on anyone.'

'But it's not just going to be you any more, is it?'

'I'll cope, I'll make sure I do. And not wanting to marry you doesn't mean that I don't want you in the baby's life. I'm here, aren't I?'

Seb sat back, a little nonplussed. His title and the castle had always meant he had enjoyed interest from a certain type of woman—and with his academic qualifications and the bestselling history books he was becomingly increasingly well known for appealed to a different type. To be honest he hadn't expected he'd have to convince anyone to marry him—he had, admittedly a little arrogantly, just expected that he would make his choice and that would be it.

Apparently Daisy hadn't got that memo.

Not that there was a reason for her to; she hadn't been raised to run a home like Hawksley, nor was she an academic type looking to become a college power couple.

'If you won't marry me then the baby will be illegitimate—I know.' He raised his hand as she opened her mouth to interrupt. 'I know that doesn't mean anything any more. But for me that's serious. I need an heir—and if the baby isn't legitimate it doesn't inherit. How will he or she feel, Daisy, if I marry someone else and they see a younger sibling inherit?'

Her face whitened. 'You'd do that?'

'If I had a younger brother then, no. But I'm the last of my family. I don't have any choice.'

'What if I can't do it?' Daisy was twisting her hands together. 'What if it's not enough for me?' She turned and picked the dishcloth back up. Her back was a little hunched, as if she were trying to keep her emotions in.

'It's a lot to give up, Seb. I always wanted what my parents have, to meet someone who completes me, who I complete.' She huffed out a short laugh. 'I know it's sentimental but when you grow up seeing that…'

'Just give it a go.' Seb was surprised by how much he wanted, needed her to say yes—and not just because of the child she carried, not just because she could solve the whole heir issue and provide the stability he needed to turn the castle's fortunes around.

But they were the important reasons and Seb ruthlessly pushed aside the memory of that night, the urge to reach out and touch her, to run a finger along those long, bare legs. 'If it doesn't work out or if you're unhappy I won't stop you leaving.'

'Divorce?' Her voice caught on the word and her back seemed to shrink inwards.

'Leave that.' He stood up and took the dishcloth from her unresisting hand, tilting her chin until she looked up at him, her eyes cloudy. 'If you wanted then yes, an amicable, friendly divorce. I hope you'll give it a real try though, promise me five years at least.'

That was a respectable amount of time; the family name had been dragged through the mud enough.

'I don't know.' She stepped back, away from his touch, and he dropped his empty hand, the silk of her skin imprinted on his fingertips. 'Getting married with a get-out clause seems wrong.'

'All marriages have a get-out clause. Look.' Seb clenched his hands. He was losing her. In a way he was impressed; he thought the title and castle was inducement enough for most women.

It was time for the big guns.

'This isn't about us. It's about our child. His future. We owe it to him to be responsible, to do the right thing for him.'

'Or her.'

'Or her.'

Thoughts were whirling around in Daisy's brain, a giant tangled skein of them. She was so tired, her limbs heavy, her shoulders slumping under the decision she was faced with.

But she was going to be a mother. What did she think that meant? All pushing swings and ice creams on the beach? She hadn't thought beyond the birth, hadn't got round to figuring out childcare and working long days on sleepless nights. It would be good to have someone else involved. Not someone she was dependent on but someone who was as invested in the baby as she was.

And if he didn't marry her he would marry elsewhere. That should make it easier to turn him down. But it showed how committed he was.

What would she tell people? That she'd messed up again? She'd worked so hard to put her past behind her. The thought of confessing the truth to her family sent her stomach into complicated knots. How could she admit to her adoring parents and indulgent sisters that she was pregnant after a one-night stand—but don't worry, she was getting married?

It wasn't the whirlwind marriage part that would send her parents into a tailspin. After all, they had known each other for less than forty-eight hours when they had walked into that Las Vegas chapel. It was the businesslike arrangement that they would disapprove of.

But maybe they didn't have to know...

'How would it work?'

He didn't hesitate. 'Family first, Hawksley second. Discretion always. I'm a private person, no magazines invited in to coo over our lovely home, no scandalous headlines.'

That made sense. A welcome kind of sense. Publicity ran through her family's veins; it would be nice to step away from that.

But her main question was still unvoiced, still unanswered. She steeled herself.

'What about intimacy?'

Seb went perfectly still apart from one muscle, beating in his cheek, his eyes darkening. Daisy took another step back, reaching for the chair as support as an answering beat pounded through her body.

'Intimacy?' His voice was low, as if the word was forced from him. 'That's up to you, Daisy. We worked—' he paused '—well together. It would be nice to have a full marriage. But that's up to you.'

Worked *well*? *Nice?* She had been thinking *spectacular*. Could she really do this? Marry someone who substituted rules for love, discretion for affection and thought respect was the pinnacle of success?

But in the circumstances how could she not? It wasn't as if she had an alternative plan.

Daisy swallowed, hard, a lump the size of a

Kardashian engagement ring forming in her throat. This was so far from her dreams, her hopes.

'I have a condition.' Was that her voice? So confident?

Seb's eyes snapped onto hers with unblinking focus. 'Name it.'

'We don't tell anyone why we're marrying like this. If we do this then we pretend. We pretend that we are head over heels ridiculously besotted. If you can do that then yes. We have a deal.'

CHAPTER THREE

'HI.'

How did one greet one's fiancé when one was a) pregnant, b) entering a marriage of convenience and c) pretending to be in love?

It should be a kiss on the cheek. Daisy greeted everyone with a kiss on the cheek, from her mother to her clients, but her stomach tumbled at the thought of pressing her lips to that stubbled cheek, inhaling the scent of leather and outdoors and soap.

Instead she stood aside, holding the door half open, her knuckles white as she clung onto the door handle as if it anchored her to the safety of her old life. 'Come in, I'm nearly ready.'

Seb stepped through and then stopped still, his eyes narrowing as he looked around slowly.

A converted loft, all exposed brickwork and steel girders, one wall dominated by five floor-to-ceiling windows through which the midday sun came flooding in. A galley kitchen at one

end, built-in shelves crammed with books, orna-
ments and knick-knacks running along the side
wall and the rest of the ground-floor space bare
except for an old blue velvet sofa, a small bistro
table and chairs and the lamps she used to light
her subjects. The bulk of her personal belongings
were on the overhanging mezzanine, which doubled as her bedroom and relaxing space.

Daisy adored her light-filled spacious studio and
yet, compared to Seb's home, steeped in history
and stuffed with antiques, her flat felt sparse and
achingly trendy.

'Nice.' Seb looked more at home than she had
thought possible, maybe because he had ditched
the fleece for a long-sleeved T-shirt in a soft grey
cotton and newer, cleaner jeans. Maybe because
he stood there confidently, unashamedly exam-
ining the room, looking at each one of the photos hung on every available bit of wall space. He
turned, slowly, taking in every detail with that
cool assessing gaze. 'Wedding photography must
pay better than I realised.'

'It's not mine unfortunately. I rent it from a
friend. An artist.' Daisy gestured over to the
massive oil seascape dominating the far wall. 'I
used to share with four other students on the floor

above and it got a little cramped—physically *and* mentally, all those artistic temperaments in one open-plan space! It was such a relief when John decided to move to Cornwall and asked if I was interested in renting the studio from him.'

'Mates' rates?'

'Not quite.' Daisy tried to swallow back her defensiveness at the assumption. Her parents would have loved to set her up in style but she had been determined to go it alone, no matter how difficult it was to find a suitable yet affordable studio. John's offer had been the perfect solution. 'I do pay rent but John's turned into a bit of a hermit so I also handle all the London side of his business for him. It works well for us both.'

'Handy. Are you leaving all that?' He nodded towards the studio lights.

'I'll still use this as my workspace.' Daisy might have agreed to move in with Seb straight away but she wasn't ready to break her ties to her old life. Not yet, not until she knew how this new world would work out. 'It's only an hour's drive. I'm all packed up. It's over here.'

It wasn't much, less than her mother took for a weekend away. A case containing her favourite cameras and lenses. Her Mac. A couple of bags filled with clothes and cosmetics. If this worked out she could move the rest of her things later: the books, prints, artwork, favourite vases and bowls. Her hat collection. How they would look in the museum-like surroundings of Hawksley Castle she couldn't begin to imagine.

Seb cast a glance at the small pile. 'Are you sure this is all you want to take? I want you to feel at home. You can make any changes you want, re-decorate, rearrange.'

'Even the library?'

His mouth quirked. 'As long as it stays warm.'

'Of course.' Daisy walked over to the hatstand at the foot of the mezzanine staircase and, after a moment's hesitation, picked up a dark pink cloche, accessorised with a diamanté brooch. It was one of her favourite hats, a car-boot-sale find. She settled it on top of her head and tugged it into place before turning to the mirror that hung behind it and coating her lips in a layer of her favourite red lipstick.

She was ready.

'First stop the registry office.' Seb had picked up both bags of clothes and Daisy swung her camera bag over her shoulder before picking up her laptop bag, her chest tight with apprehension.

She swivelled and looked back at the empty space. *You'll be back tomorrow*, she told herself, but stepping out of the front door still felt momentous, not just leaving her home but a huge step into the unknown.

Deep breath, don't cry and lock the door. Her stomach swooped as if it were dropping sixty storeys at the speed of light but she fought it, managing to stop her hand from trembling as she double-locked the door.

Did Seb have similar doubts? If so he hid them well; he was the epitome of calm as they exited the building and walked to the car. He had brought one of the estate Land Rovers ready to transport her stuff; it might be parked with the other North London four-by-fours but its mud-splattered bumpers and utilitarian inside proclaimed it country bumpkin. She doubted any of its gleaming, leather-interior neighbours ever saw anything but urban roads and motorways.

'Once we have registered we have to wait sixteen days. At least we don't have to worry about a venue. The Tudor hall is licensed and I don't allow weekday weddings so we can get married—' he pulled out his phone '—two weeks on Friday. Do you want to invite anyone?' He dropped his phone back into his pocket, opening the car door and hefting her bags into the boot.

Daisy was frozen, one arm protectively around her camera bag. How could he sound so matter-of-fact? They were talking about their wedding. About commitment and promises and joining together. Okay, they were practically strangers but it should still mean something.

'Can we make it three weeks? Just to make sure? Plus I want my parents and sisters there and I need to give Rose enough notice to get back from New York.'

'You want your whole family to come?' He held the door open for her, a faint look of surprise on his face.

Daisy put one foot on the step, hesitated and turned to face him. 'You promised we would at least pretend this was a real marriage. Of course my family needs to be there.' This was non-negotiable.

'Fine.'

Daisy's mouth had been open, ready to argue her point and she was taken aback at his one-word agreement, almost disappointed by his acquiescence. He was so calm about everything. What was going on underneath the surface? Maybe she'd never find out. She stood for a second, gaping, before closing her mouth with a snap and climbing into the passenger seat. Seb closed the door behind her and a moment later he swung himself into the driver's seat and started the engine.

Daisy wound her window down a little then leant back against the headrest watching as Seb navigated the narrow streets, taking her further and further from her home.

Married in just over three weeks. A whirlwind romance, that was what people would think; that was what she would tell them.

'That was a deep sigh.'

'Sorry, it's just...' She hesitated, pulling down the sun visor to check the angle of her hat, feeling oddly vulnerable at the thought of telling him something personal. 'I always knew exactly how I wanted my wedding to be. I know it's silly, that they were just daydreams...' With all the changes happening right now, mourning the loss of her ideal wedding seemed ridiculously self-indulgent.

'Beach at sunset? Swanky hotel? Westminster Abbey and Prince Harry in a dress uniform?'

'No, well, only sometimes.' She stole a glance

at him. His eyes were focused on the road ahead and somehow the lack of eye contact made it easier to admit just how many plans she had made. She could picture it so clearly. 'My parents live just down the lane from the village church. I always thought I'd get married there, walk to my wedding surrounded by my family and then afterwards walk back hand in hand with my new husband and have a garden party. Nothing too fancy, although Dad's band would play, of course.'

'Of course.' But he was smiling.

Daisy bit her lip as the rest of her daydream slid through her mind like an internal movie. She would be in something lacy, straight, deceptively simple. The sun would shine casting a golden glow over the soft Cotswold stone. And she would be complete.

There had been a faint ache in her chest since the day before, a swelling as if her heart were bruised. As the familiar daydream slipped away the ache intensified, her heart hammering. She was doing the right thing. Wasn't she?

It's not just about you any more, she told herself as firmly as possible.

She just wished she had had a chance to talk her options over with someone else. But who?

Her sisters? They would immediately go into emergency-planning mode, try and take over, alternately scolding her and coddling her, reducing her back to a tiresome little girl in the process.

Her parents? But no, she still had her pride if nothing else. Daisy swallowed hard, wincing at the painful lump in her throat. She had worked so hard to make up for the mistakes of her past, worked so hard to be independent from her family, to show them that she was as capable as they were. How could she tell them that she was pregnant by a man she hardly knew?

Her parents would swing into damage-limitation mode. Want her to come back home, to buy her a house, to throw money at her as if that would make everything okay. And it would be so easy to let them.

Daisy sagged in her seat. She couldn't tell them, she wouldn't tell them, but all she wanted to hear was her dad's comforting drawl and step into her mother's embrace. She didn't allow herself that luxury very often.

'Actually, can we go to the registrar's tomorrow? I don't feel comfortable registering until we have told my parents. Would you mind if we visit them first?'

Daisy waited, her hands slippery with tense anticipation. It had been so long since she had consulted with someone else or needed consensus on any action.

'Of course.' Seb took his eyes from the road for one brief second, resting them appraisingly on her hands, twisting in her lap. 'But if we're going to tell your parents we're engaged we should probably stop at a jeweller's on the way. You need a ring.'

'Daisy! Darling, what a lovely surprise.'

It was strange being face to face with someone as familiar, as famous as Sherry Huntingdon: model, muse and sometime actress. Her tall willowy figure, as taut and slender at over fifty as it had been at twenty, the blonde hair sweeping down her back seemingly as natural as her daughter's.

'And who's this?' The famously sleepy blue eyes were turned onto Seb, an unexpectedly shrewdly appraising look in them. Maybe not that unexpected—you didn't stay at the top of your profession for over thirty years without brains as well as beauty.

'Sebastian Beresford.' He held his hand out and

Daisy's mother took it, slanting a look at him from under long black lashes.

'What a treat.' Her voice was low, almost a purr. 'Daisy so seldom brings young men home. Come on in, the pair of you. Violet's around somewhere and Rick's in his studio—the Benefit Concert is creeping up on us again. Daisy, darling, you will be here to take some photos, won't you?'

'Wouldn't miss it.' Daisy linked her arm through her mother's as they walked along the meandering path that led from the driveway around the house. It was a beautiful ivy-covered house, large by any standards—unless one happened to live in a castle—dating back to William and Mary with two gracefully symmetrical wings flanking the three-storey main building.

Unlike Hawksley it had been sympathetically updated and restored and, as they rounded the corner, Seb could see tennis courts in the distance and a cluster of stable buildings and other outbuildings all evidently restored and in use.

An unexpected stab of nostalgic pain hit him. Hawksley should have been as well cared for but his grandfather had taken a perverse pride in the discomfort of the crumbling building—and as for Seb's father... He pushed the thought away, fists clenched with the unwanted anger that still flooded through him whenever he thought about his father's criminal negligence.

Sherry came to a stop as they reached a large paved terrace with steps leading upwards to the French doors at the back of the house. Comfortably padded wooden furniture was arranged to take the best advantage of the gorgeous views. 'I think it's warm enough to sit outside.' Sherry smiled at her daughter. 'I'll go get Rick. He'll be so happy to see you, Daisy. He was saying the other day we see more of Rose and she lives in New York. You two make yourselves at home. Then we can have a drink. Daisy, darling, let Vi know you're here, will you?'

'I'll text her.' Daisy perched on a bench as she pulled out her phone and, after a moment's hesitation, Seb joined her. Of course they would sit together. In fact, they should be holding hands. He looked at her long, slender fingers flying over the phone's surface and willed himself to casually reach over and slip his own fingers through hers.

Just one touch. And yet it felt more binding than the ring he had bought her and the vows he was prepared to make.

'That's Dad's studio.' Daisy slipped the phone

back into her dress pocket and pointed at the largest of the outbuildings. 'The first thing he did was convert it into a soundproofed, state-of-the-art recording studio—we were never allowed in unsupervised but it didn't stop us trying to make our own records. They weren't very good. None of us are particularly musical, much to Dad's disgust. The room next to it is used as rehearsal space and we turned the orangery into a pool and gym, otherwise we pretty much left the house as it was. It hasn't changed much since it was built.'

But it had. The paintwork was fresh, the soft furnishings and wallpaper new, the furniture chosen with care. New money in an old building. It was what Hawksley needed, if only his great-great-grandfather had married an American heiress.

'Have you lived here long?'

'Mum grew up here, her uncle is a baronet and somewhere along the family tree we descend from William Fourth, although not through the legitimate line. So, you see—' Daisy threw him a provocative smile '—you're not marrying beneath you.'

'I didn't think I was.' Seb knew very well that his blood was as red as anyone else's. It wasn't

Daisy's ancestry that worried him, it was her upbringing. If she had been brought up in a place as lavishly luxurious as Huntingdon Hall how would she cope with the draughty inconveniences of his grand and ancient home?

'Daisy? You *are* alive. Rose was trying to persuade me to break into your apartment and recover your dead body. A whole week with no word from you?'

'Vi!' Daisy jumped to her feet, sprinting up the stone steps and flinging her arms around the speaker. 'What do you mean? I texted you both! Every day.'

'Texts, anyone can send a text that says I'm fine, talk soon. But—' she eyed Seb coolly over Daisy's shoulder '—I can see you've been busy.'

Seb stood and held out his hand. 'You must be Violet.' A meaningful glare from Daisy reminded him of his role. 'Daisy has told me so much about you.' He walked forward and slipped an arm around Daisy, ignoring the electricity that snaked up his arm from the exact spot where his fingers curled around her slender waist. Daisy started, just a little, at his touch before inhaling and leaning into him, her body pliant, moulding into his side as if she belonged there.

'Really? She hasn't mentioned you at all.' Violet took his outstretched hand in her cool grasp for a moment. 'She usually tells me everything.' Her eyes were narrowed as she assessed him. It was more than a little disconcerting to be so comprehensively overlooked even by such very blue eyes.

The family resemblance was striking. Violet was a little taller, a little curvier than her younger sister and her heart-shaped face gave nothing away, unlike Daisy's all too telling features, but she had the Huntingdon colouring, the high cheekbones and the same mane of golden hair.

That was as far as the resemblance went; Daisy was wearing a monochrome print dress, the bodice tight fitting and the skirt flaring out to just above her knees, a dark pink short cardigan slung over her shoulders and the carefully positioned hat finishing off the outfit with a quirky flourish. Violet, by contrast, was sensibly clad in jeans and a white shirt, her hair held back from her face by a large slide, her make-up understated and demure.

'Not everything.' Daisy flushed. 'I am twenty-four, you know. I do have some secrets.'

'Daisy-Waisy, you never managed to keep a secret in your whole life.' Violet grinned at her sister with obvious affection. Her eyes cooled as she returned to assessing Seb. 'And what is it that you do?'

For one, almost irresistible moment Seb had the urge to emulate his grandfather, draw himself up to his full six feet one, look down at Violet and drawl, 'Do? My good woman, I don't *do*. I am. Earl of Holgate to be precise,' just to shake her cool complacency. He didn't need Daisy's warning pinch to resist. 'I manage a large estate. That's where we met. Daisy was working there.'

'He came to my rescue.' The face upturned to his was so glowing Seb nearly forgot they were acting. 'I was snowed in and he rescued me. It was super romantic, Vi.'

'Words no father wants to hear.' Seb started at the deep American drawl and hurriedly turned.

'Dad.' Daisy tugged Seb down the steps, almost running. She slipped out of Seb's grasp and threw her arms around the slight man on the terrace.

'Missed you, Daisy girl. How's that camera of yours?'

'Busy, I already promised Mum I would cover the Benefit Concert but if you want some promo shots doing beforehand just ask. Formal, informal, you choose.'

'I'll ask Rose. She makes all those kinds of decisions. So who is this romantic knight you've brought home?' Rick Cross turned to Seb with an appraising gaze.

For the third time in five minutes Seb stood still as he was examined by keen eyes. Lucky Daisy, having such a loving, protective family. She didn't need to marry him at all; they would close ranks and take care of her. If he wanted to raise his heir he'd better keep his side of their strange bargain.

'Sebastian Beresford. It's an honour to meet you, sir.' Seb managed, just, not to blurt out that Rick Cross had made one of the first CDs he had ever bought. A CD he had listened to over and over again.

Daisy's father was so familiar it seemed odd that he was a stranger; the craggy face, wild hair and skinny frame were timeless. Rick Cross had burst onto the music scene at twenty and never left. Age had definitely not withered him; he still toured, released and dominated the headlines although these days it was philanthropy not wild antics that kept him there.

'Beresford? I've read your books. Good to meet you.'

Daisy slipped an arm around Seb and he obediently held her close as she beamed at her family.

'We've got some news. Mum, Dad, Vi. Seb and I are engaged. We're going to get married!'

It was exhausting, pretending. Hanging on Seb's arm, smiling, showing off the admittedly beautiful but somewhat soulless solitaire on her third finger as her family crowded around with congratulations and calls for champagne.

A glass of champagne Daisy pretended to sip. If her parents suspected for one single second the real reason for her marriage they would be so disappointed. Not in her, for her.

And she absolutely couldn't bear that. To let them down again.

They knew how much she wanted to fall in love, to be loved.

Vi hung back a little, her eyes suspicious even as her mouth smiled. Her sister had been so badly burned, it was hard for her to trust. And Daisy was lying after all.

'I'll call the vicar right away.' Her mother had swung into action with alarming haste. 'You'll want spring naturally, Daisy darling, next year or the year after? I think next year. A long engagement is so dreadfully dreary.'

Daisy looked at Seb for help but he had been

drawn into a conversation with her father about guitar chords. Did Seb know anything about guitars or chords? She had no idea.

No idea what his favourite food was, his favourite memory, band, song, poem, book, film, TV programme. If he played a musical instrument, liked to run, watched football, rugby or both...

'Daisy, stop daydreaming,' her mother scolded as she had so many times before. 'Next year, darling?'

Daisy tugged her hat back into place. 'Sorry.' She put on her widest smile and did her best to look as if her heart weren't shattering into ever smaller fragments with every word. 'We're not getting married here.'

The rest of her family fell silent and Daisy could feel three sets of eyes boring into her. 'Not getting married here?'

'It's all you have ever wanted.'

'Don't be silly, Daisy girl. Where else would you get married?'

'It's my fault, I'm afraid.' Seb had stepped behind her and Daisy leant back into the lean, hard body with a hastily concealed sob of relief. 'I, ah, I own a licensed property and we rather thought we would get married there. I hope you're not too disappointed.'

'A licensed venue?' Vi, of course. 'Like a pub?'

'No, well, actually yes, there is a pub in the village. It's a tied village, so technically it belongs to me but I don't run it.'

So much for Seb rescuing her, although Daisy would bet her favourite lens that Mr Darcy would quail faced with her entire family. If Rose were here as well to complete the interrogation then Seb would be running for the hills, his precious heir forgotten.

'Seb owns Hawksley Castle, we're getting married there and it won't be next spring.' It was time to act as she had never acted before. Daisy nuzzled in closer to Seb, one arm around his neck, and kissed him. Just a short, quick kiss, his mouth hard under hers.

Heat shimmered through her, low and intense and she quivered, grabbing for words to hide behind, hoping Seb hadn't noticed how he had affected her. 'We're getting married this month, in just over three weeks. Excited?'

'Why the rush?' Vi's eyes flickered over Daisy's belly and she resisted the urge to breathe in.

'Why not?' Keeping her voice as light and insouciant as possible, Daisy pressed even closer to Seb, his arm tight around her. It might just be for show but she was grateful for the support both physically and mentally. 'After all, Mum and Dad, what do you always say? When you know, you know. You only knew each other for a weekend before you got married.'

'But, Daisy, darling that was the late seventies and we were in Vegas.'

'It's true though, honey.' Rick Cross's voice had softened to the besotted tones he still used whenever he spoke to his wife, the intimate voice that excluded everyone else, even their three daughters. 'We only needed that weekend to know we were meant to be. Maybe Daisy girl has been as lucky as we were?'

The ever-present ache intensified. 'I am, Dad. Be happy for me?'

'Of course we are. Hawksley, eh? I met your father once. Remember, Sherry? On Mustique. Now that was a man who liked to party. Talking of which, we've finished the champagne. Let's go in and get some more and toast this thing properly. I might have some photos of that holiday, Seb.'

Her parents bore Seb off up the steps, both talking nineteen to the dozen. Daisy stood for a moment, watching. In nearly every way this was the image from her dreams: a handsome, eligible man, her parents' approval.

A man she barely knew. A man who didn't love her. A man who might have a comforting embrace and a mouth she melted against but who wanted a businesslike, emotion-free marriage.

'You don't have to rush into this. How long have you known him?' Vi had also stayed behind. Her arms were folded as she waited for Daisy to answer.

'Six weeks.' This at least wasn't a lie. 'And I'm not rushing into anything. I want to do this, Vi. Be happy for me.' She smiled coaxingly at her sister.

'I want to be.' Vi stared at her, worry in her eyes. 'It's just, I heard rumours. Daisy, Hawksley Castle is beautiful but it's expensive and his parents spent a lot. More than a lot. Are you sure he's not…?' She paused.

'Not what?' But she knew. 'After my fortune? I don't have a fortune, Vi!'

'No, but Daddy does and you know it drives him mad we won't live off him. He'd do anything for you, Daise, even prop up a money pit like Hawksley.'

If Daisy knew anything about Seb it was this:

she could hand on heart acquit him of any interest in her father's money. The shock in his eyes when he'd found out who she was had been utterly genuine. But Vi was right to be suspicious; they were deceiving her.

And yet anger was simmering, slow, hot, intense. 'Seb does not need my non-existent fortune or Daddy to bail him out. He's working every waking hour to turn Hawksley around his way and he'll do it too. So butt out, Vi. And no running to Rose either. Let her make her own mind up.'

Where had that come from?

Vi looked at her searchingly. 'Okay, Daise, calm down. I won't say anything. Let's go in and I'll get to know your Seb properly. My little sister's marrying an earl. You always did like to show off.'

'I didn't know he was an earl when I met him!' But Vi just laughed and pulled her up the steps and into the vast kitchen diner that dominated the back of the house.

'There you are, darling. Three weeks! That's no time at all to plan. We need to get started right now. How many people can you seat? There will be rooms at the castle for the family, I suppose? Colour scheme yellow and white, of course.'

'Great!' Violet scowled. 'So I get lumbered with

light purple and Rose gets almost any colour she wants.'

'I could have called you Marigold, just think about that,' her mother said. 'We need to go shopping right away, Daisy. And discuss menus, and cakes and do you think Grandpa will come?'

'The thing is, Mum…' Daisy took a deep breath. 'I don't need any of those things. It's going to be very small. Just us, and Rose, of course, if she can come. So no colour scheme needed. We could have cake though.'

'No!' Daisy jumped at the autocratic note in her mother's voice. It wasn't a note she heard often; her parents were indulgent to the point of spoiling their girls. Rose always said that was why they had sent them to such a strict boarding school, so that someone else would do the hard parts and they could just enjoy their daughters.

'No, Daisy. Not this time.'

This time? Daisy stared at her mother in confusion. 'I…'

She didn't get a chance to continue. Sherry's voice rose higher. 'You wanted to leave home in your teens? Your father and I respected that. We were both working at eighteen after all. You won't allow us to pay your rent or buy you a car or help you in any way? I don't like it but I accept it. You visit once in a blue moon? I tell myself that at least you text us and I can follow you on Twitter.'

The heat burned high on Daisy's cheeks. It hadn't really occurred to her that her parents would interpret her need to go it alone as rejection. She held up a hand, whether in defence or supplication she didn't know.

It made no difference; her mother had hit her stride. 'You want to get married in less than a month? Fine. You want to get married away from home? No problem. But you will *not* have a tiny wedding. I know you, you've dreamt of a big, beautiful wedding since you were tiny and that, my girl, is exactly what you are going to have. You are going to let me pay for it and, young lady, nobody—' the blue eyes flashed '—*nobody* is going to stop me organising it for you.'

CHAPTER FOUR

'I'M SO SORRY.' Daisy hadn't said much as they drove the sixty miles back to Hawksley Castle but she straightened once Seb turned the Land Rover down the track that led to the castle. 'I should have planned the visit—gone on my own, maybe. I know you don't want any fuss.'

Seb slid a gaze her way. She was pale, the red lipstick bitten away. 'We could just say no.' We. It felt odd saying the word, like putting on somebody else's sock.

'We could.' Daisy slumped further down into the seat and sighed. 'But then they'd know something was up. I may have mentioned my dream wedding plans once or twice.'

He'd bet she had, he already knew far too many details about Daisy's Dream Wedding. Details imparted by eager parents and a grim-faced sister all determined that she should have her Big Day. 'Tell them I'm allergic to the thought. Cold sweats, clammy hands and hives. Or that small is more romantic and they're lucky we're not eloping.'

She didn't respond and at her silence an unwelcome thought crept into his mind; was he being presumptuous? Starting off this unconventional marriage by trampling over his prospective wife's wishes. Great start. 'Unless you want this?'

'I thought I did.' Her voice was wistful. 'But that was before...'

A stab of something that felt uncomfortably like guilt pierced him. She hadn't sought this out. His carelessness had thrust it upon her—the least he could do was allow her to have her way on this one small thing, even if the thought of all that attention did make his stomach churn, his hands clammy on the steering wheel.

Seb inhaled. To make this work meant compromise on both sides. He needed to start somewhere. 'We could rearrange. Your house, your church, garden party—the whole shebang if it means that much to you.'

'Really?' Her face brightened for one second and then it was gone, as if the spark had never been. 'No, thank you for offering, I do really appreciate it but it's fine. That wedding was a dream, a romance. It would feel—' she hesitated '—even more fake if I made you go along with my silly dreams. Here will be much more appropriate. But would you mind, if we did accommodate Mum a little and allow her to help? I'll keep it under control, I promise.'

'Of course. This is your wedding and your home.' The words slid out easily even as his chest constricted. How would this pampered butterfly manage in a place as unwieldy and stately as Hawksley? But what choice did he have? Did either of them have? They had made their bed…

He braked as he slid the car into the parking space and turned to face her. 'Look, Daisy, I really think this can work. If we're honest with each other, if we keep communicating.'

She was staring down at her hands, her lashes dark as they shadowed her eyes. 'You don't think we are rushing into it?'

Seb couldn't help the corner of his mouth curving up. 'Not at all. I believe several of my ancestors only met their spouse on their wedding day. We'll have had at least two months between meeting and wedding—a shocking amount of time.'

There was no responsive smile. 'I still think there would be no harm in waiting until after we've had a scan and know more. It's still such early days. I haven't even been to the doctor's yet. If we marry and I am just ten weeks along there's still a chance something could go wrong. We'd be trapped in a marriage neither of us want with no baby! What would we do then?'

She made sense, every word made sense and the sensible side of Seb acknowledged the truth of it, welcomed the truth of it—and yet something in him recoiled.

'There are no certainties anywhere. If it goes wrong then we mourn. We mourn and regroup. Daisy…' He reached over and took one of her hands; it lay unresisting in his, the long slender fingers cold. 'I can't see into the future and, yes, in some ways you are right. We can wait, for the scan, wait till sixteen weeks or even thirty weeks. Or we can take a leap of faith. That's what marriage is. Ours is just a bigger leap.'

He thought about it for a moment. 'Or a shorter one. Our eyes are open after all.'

She looked straight at him, her eyes wide and troubled. 'I'm only agreeing to an early marriage so my family doesn't find out I'm pregnant, so they don't try and talk me out of it. They know how important marriage is to me, how important love is. What about you? Why don't you want to wait?'

Seb squeezed his eyes shut. He could still hear them, his parents' vicious arguments, their exuberant reconciliations. He thought about brushing her off but if he wanted this to work then he needed to be honest. Needed her to understand what he was offering—and what he could never give her.

'My mother didn't want a baby. She didn't want to ruin her figure with pregnancy, didn't want to stop partying, didn't want to go through labour. But she did want to be a countess and an heir was part of the deal. She told me once, when she was drunk, how happy she had been when they said I was a boy so that she didn't have to go through it all again. That if it was up to her she would have remained childless.'

I had you because I had no choice. It was the worst year of my life.

'Luckily there were grandparents, schools, nannies. She could at least pretend to be child-free—except when it suited her. I don't want our child to think that, to feel like a burden. I want to welcome him or her into the world with open arms and make sure he or she knows that they were wanted. Because we may not have planned it but I do want it—and you do too. That's why it matters, that they are born with all the ridiculous privileges this title gives them. That's why it matters that we marry.'

She didn't say anything for a long moment but her fingers closed over his, strength in her cool grasp. 'Okay,' she said finally. 'Three weeks on Friday it is. Let's go and see the registrar tomorrow morning and get booked in. I guess I should register with a doctor nearby as well.'

'Good.' He returned the pressure, relieved. At her acquiescence. At her silent understanding. 'Are you tired or do you want the full guided tour of your new home?'

'Are you kidding? A personal guided tour from the hot prof himself? Show me everything.'

'So this is the Norman keep. Family legend has it that a knight, Sir William Belleforde, came over with the invasion in 1066 and was granted these lands. During the next few centuries the name was anglicised and corrupted to Beresford. He built the keep.'

'Cosy.' Daisy pivoted, looking about her at the dark grey walls built out of blocks of grey stone, the narrow window slits. She pulled her cardigan closer as the wind whistled through the tower. 'Was this it?'

'There was a wooden castle attached but this was the main defensive base and would have been quite roomy. There were three floors inside here—look, there's the old staircase. There was also a fortified wall around the rest of the castle. When you visit the village you'll see that many of the older houses are built with the stone from the walls.'

Daisy tilted her head back, trying to imagine one thousand years away. 'Walls, battlements, arrow slits. Nothing says home like defensive buildings. Were there many battles here?'

Seb shook his head. 'There was very little fighting here even during the Wars of the Roses and the Civil War. My ancestors were too canny to get involved.'

'No Cavalier ghosts trailing along with their heads under their arms?' Obviously this was a relief and yet didn't a house like this deserve a few ghosts?

'Not a one. We changed our religion to suit the Tudors and the colour of our roses for the Plantagenets. You'll be glad to hear that an impetuous younger son did go to France with Charles II and when he inherited the title he was made first Earl of Holgate. Although some say that was because his wife was one of the King's many mistresses—with her Lord's consent.'

'Good to know she was doing her bit for the family's advancement. Is that still a requirement for the countess? I'm not sure I'm up to it if so!'

He shot her a wry smile. 'I'm glad to hear it. No, I'm more than happy with the earldom, no favours for advancements required. Of course by then the keep was abandoned as a home. It was already un-used by the late fourteenth century and the Great Hall was built around one hundred years later.'

He led her out of the chill stone building and swung open the huge oak door that led into the Tudor part of the castle.

Daisy had spent an entire day in this part of the castle, photographing a wedding. It had felt com-pletely different with long tables set out, the dais at the far end filled with a top table, the candle-like iron chandeliers blazing with light. 'I can see why they moved in here. It may be large but it's a lot warmer. Having a working roof is a definite advantage. A floor is helpful too.'

'Especially when you let the place out,' he

agreed. 'Brides can be a bit precious about things like dirt floors and holes in the roof.'

'It's in incredible condition.' She had taken so many photos of the details: the carvings on the panelling, the way the huge beams curved.

'It has to be. We couldn't hold events here if not. It may look untouched since Elizabethan times but there is electricity throughout, working toilets and a fully kitted-out kitchen through that door. In fact, this is more up to date than parts of the main house. It's always been used as a ballroom, which made the decision to hire it out a little easier.' He winced. 'My grandfather thought we had a duty to share the castle with the wider world, but not for profit.'

'Hence the restrictive opening hours?'

'Absolutely. I don't know what he would say if he saw the weddings. They're not making enough of a difference though, even though I charge an obscene amount. I'm trying to work out how to make the castle self-funding and yet keep it as a home. Keep the heart of it intact. It's not easy.'

'You're planning to stay here, then, not live in Oxford?'

'Now it's mine? Yes. I can stay in college if I need to, although it will be strange, commuting in after all these years. It's like being pulled constantly in two different directions, between the demands of my career and the demands of my home—they both need all of my time or so it seems. But a place like this? It's a privilege to own it, to be the one taking care of it.'

His eyes lit up with enthusiasm, the rather severe features relaxing as he pointed out another interesting architectural feature and recounted yet another bit of family history that Daisy was convinced he made up on the spot. Nobody could have such a scandalous family tree—rakes and highwaymen and runaway brides in every generation.

'You really love it, don't you?'

'How could I not? Growing up here, it was like living in my own time machine. I could be anybody from Robin Hood to Dick Turpin.'

'Always the outlaw?'

'They seemed to have the most fun. Had the horses, the adoration, got the girls.'

'All the important things in life.'

'Exactly.' He grinned; it made him look more boyish. More desirable. Daisy's breath hitched in her throat, her mouth suddenly dry.

Their gazes caught, snagged, and they stood

there for a long moment, neither moving. His eyes darkened to an impenetrable green, a hint of something dangerous flickering at their core and awareness shivered down Daisy's spine. She moved backwards, just a few centimetres, almost propelled by the sheer force of his gaze until her back hit the wooden panelling. She leant against it, thankful for the support, her legs weak.

She was still caught in his gaze, warmth spreading out from her abdomen, along her limbs, her skin buzzing where his eyes rested on her, the memory of his touch skittering along her nerves. Nervous, she licked her lips, the heat in her body intensifying as she watched his eyes move to her mouth, recognised the hungry expression in them.

He wanted a working marriage. A full marriage.

Right now, that seemed like the only thing that made sense in this whole tangled mess.

He took a step closer. And another. Daisy stayed still, almost paralysed by the purposeful intent in his face, her pulse hammering an insistent beat of need, of want at every pressure point in her body, pressure, a sweet, aching swelling in her chest.

'Seb?' It was almost a plea, almost a sob, a cry for something, an end to the yearning that so suddenly and so fiercely gripped her.

He paused, his eyes still on her and then one last step. So close and yet still, still not touching even though her body was crying out for contact, pulled towards him by the magnetism of sheer need. He leant, just a little, a hand on either side of her, braced against the wall.

He still hadn't touched her.

They remained perfectly still, separated by mere millimetres, their eyes locked, heat flickering between them, the wait stoking it higher and higher. He had to kiss her, had to or she would spontaneously combust. He had to press that hard mouth against hers, allow those skilled hands to roam, to know her again. To fulfil her again. He had to.

Daisy jumped as a tune blared out from her pocket, a jaunty folk cover of one of her father's greatest hits. Seb's hands dropped and he retreated just a few steps as she fumbled for it, half ready to sob with frustration, half relieved. She hadn't even moved in yet and she was what? Begging him to kiss her?

Very businesslike.

Hands damp, she pulled out the phone and stared at the screen, unable to focus. Pressing the button, she held it shakily to her ear. 'Hello?'

'Daisy? You *are* alive, then?'

'Rose!' Daisy smiled apologetically at Seb and turned slightly, as if not seeing him would give her some privacy, her heart still hammering.

'Vi said I had to call you right now. Where have you been? Not cool to go offline with no warning, little sis, not cool at all.'

It was what, four o'clock in the afternoon? It felt later, as if several days, not just a few hours, had passed since she had woken up in her own bed, in her own flat for the last time. It would still be morning in New York. She pictured her sister, feet on the desk, a coffee by her hand, an incorrigible mixture of efficiency, impatience and effortless style.

'Things have been a bit crazy.' Daisy knew she sounded breathless, welcomed it. Hopefully her sister would put it down to girlish excitement not a mixture of frustration and embarrassment. 'Rose, I have some news. I'm engaged!'

There was a long silence at the end of the phone. Then: 'But you're not even dating anyone. It's not Edwin, is it? I thought you said he was dull.'

'No, of course it's not Edwin!' Daisy could feel her cheeks heating. 'We split up months ago, and he's not dull exactly,' she added loyally. 'Just a little precise. It's Seb, Sebastian Beresford, you know, Rose, he wrote that book on Charles II's illegitimate children you loved so much.'

'The hot professor? England's answer to Indiana Jones?' The shriek was so loud that Daisy was convinced Seb could hear it through the phone. 'How on earth did you meet him, Daisy? What kind of parties are you going to nowadays? Dinner parties? Academic soirées?' Rose laughed.

There it was, unspoken but insinuated. How could silly little Daisy with barely a qualification to her name have anything in common with a lauded academic?

'Through work,' she said a little stiffly. 'He owns Hawksley Castle.'

'Of course,' her sister breathed. 'Didn't he just inherit a title? What is he, a baron?'

'An earl.' It sounded ludicrous just saying the words. She could feel Seb's sardonic gaze on her and turned around so her back was entirely towards him, wishing she had gone outside to have this awkward conversation.

'An earl?' Rose went off into another peal of laughter. Daisy held the phone away from her ear, waiting for her sister to calm down. 'Seriously? This isn't you and Vi winding me up?'

Was it that implausible? Daisy didn't want to hear the answer.

'It's true.'

'Well, I suppose I had better meet him if you're going to marry him. I'll be over for the Benefit Concert in about four weeks. There's only so much I can do this side of the Atlantic. With the tour on top of everything else I am completely snowed under. I can't cope with one more thing at the moment.' Rose was in charge of all their parents' PR as well as organising the annual Benefit Concert their father did for charity. His decision to take the band back on tour had added even more to her sister's already heavy workload.

So she was going to love the last-minute changes to her plan. 'Actually you're going to meet him sooner than that. We're getting married in three weeks and you have to be my bridesmaid, Rose. You will be there, won't you?'

'What? When? But why, Daisy? What's the rush?'

'No rush,' she replied, hating that she was lying to her family. 'We don't want to wait, that's all.'

There was a deep sigh at the other end of the telephone. 'Daise, you know what you're like. You always go all in at first. You thought you'd found

The One at sixteen for goodness' sake, and again when you were at St Martin's. Then there was Edwin—you told me you were soulmates. Then you wake up one day and realise that they're actually frogs, not your prince. Nice frogs—but still frogs. What makes this one different? Apart from the amazing looks, the keen brain and the title, of course.'

Daisy wanted to slide down onto the floor and stay there. Her family had always teased her about her impetuous romantic nature. But to have it recited back to her like that. It made her sound so young. So stupid.

But Rose was wrong. This wasn't like the others. She was under no illusions that Seb was her soulmate. She wasn't in love.

'This is different and when you meet him you'll understand.' She hoped she sounded convincing—it was the truth after all.

'Okay.' Rose sighed. 'If you say it's different this time then I believe you.'

What Rose actually meant was that she would phone Vi and get her opinion and then the two of them could close ranks and sit in judgement on Daisy. Just as they always did.

'You will be there though, won't you, Rosy

Posy?' Daisy wheedled using the old pet name her sister affected to despise. 'I can't get married without you.' Her breath hitched and she heard the break in her voice. Her sisters might be bossy and annoying and have spent most of their childhood telling her to leave them alone but they were hers. And she needed them.

'Of course I'll be there, silly. I'll make the rings, my gift to you both. Send me his finger size, okay?'

'Okay.' Daisy clung onto the phone, wishing her sister were there, wishing she could tell her the truth.

'I have to go. There are a million and one things to do. Talk soon. Call me if you need anything.'

'I will. Bye.'

Daisy clicked the phone shut, oddly bereft as the connection cut. Rose had been abroad for so long—and when she did come home she worked.

'That was my other sister.'

Seb was leaning against the wall, arms folded, one ankle crossed over the other. 'I guessed.'

'She makes rings, as a hobby although she's so good she should do it professionally. She's offered to make ours so I need to send your finger size over.'

She half expected him to say he wasn't going to wear a ring and relief filled her as he nodded acquiescence. 'Why doesn't she—do it professionally?'

It was a good question. Why didn't she? Daisy struggled to find the right words. 'She's good at PR. Mummy and Daddy have always relied on her, and on Vi, to help them. They're so incredibly busy and it's easier to keep it in the family, with people they trust.' Her loving, indulgent, generous but curiously childlike parents.

'What about you? What do you do?'

'Me? I take photos. That's all I'm good for. They don't need me for anything else.' She couldn't keep the bitterness out of her voice.

He looked her curiously. 'That's not the impression I got today. They were bowled over to see you, all fatted calves and tears of joy.'

'That's because I don't go home enough.' The guilt gnawed away at her. 'I don't involve them in my life. It drives my mum crazy as you can probably tell. She doesn't trust me not to mess up without her.'

'Why not?'

Daisy looked at him sharply but the question

seemed genuine enough. She sighed. 'It always took me twice as long as my sisters to do anything,' she admitted. 'I was a late talker, walker, reader. My handwriting was atrocious, I hated maths—I was always in trouble at school for talking or messing around.'

'You and half the population.'

'But half the population don't have Rose and Violet as older sisters,' she pointed out. 'I don't think I had a single teacher who didn't ask me why I couldn't be more like my sisters. Why my work wasn't the same standard, my manners as good. By the time I was expelled that narrative was set in stone. I was like the family kitten— cute enough but you couldn't expect much from me. Of course actually being expelled didn't help.'

'It must have been difficult.'

'It was humiliating.' Looking back, that was what she remembered most clearly. How utterly embarrassed she had been. 'It was all over the papers. People were commiserating with my parents as if my life was finished. At sixteen! So Mum and Dad tried to do what they do best. Spend money on me and paper over the cracks. They offered to send me to finishing school, or for Mum to set me up with her modelling agency. I could be a social-ite or a model. I wasn't fit for anything else.'

'But you're not either of those things.'

'I refused.' She swallowed. 'I think the worst part was that the whole family treated the whole incident like a joke. They didn't once ask me how I felt, what I wanted to do. To be. I heard Dad say to Mum that I was never going to pass any exams anyway so did it really matter.' She paused, try-ing not to let that painful memory wind her the way it usually did.

It had hurt knowing that even her own parents didn't have faith in her.

'I didn't want them to fix it. I wanted to fix it myself. So I went to the local college and then art school. I left home properly in my first term and never went back. I needed to prove to them, to me, that they don't have to take care of me.' She laughed but there was no humour in her voice. 'Look how well that's turned out.'

'I think you do just fine by yourself.'

'Pregnant after a one-night stand?' She shook her head. 'Maybe they're right.'

'Pregnant? Yes. But you faced up to it, came here and told me, which was pretty damn brave.

You're sacrificing your own dreams for the baby. I think that makes you rather extraordinary.'

'Oh, well.' She shrugged, uncomfortable with the compliments. 'I do get to be a countess and sleep with a king for social advantage after all.'

'There is that.' His eyes had darkened again. 'Where were we, when your sister phoned and interrupted us?'

Daisy felt it again, that slow sensual tug towards him, the hyper awareness of his every move, the tilt of his mouth, the gleam of his eye, the play of muscle in his shoulders.

'You were telling me about wanting to be an outlaw.' She felt it but she wasn't going there. Not today, not when she was in such an emotional tumult.

'Coward.' The word was soft, silky, full of promise. Then he straightened, the intentness gone. 'So I was. Ready to see the rest of your home? Let's zoom forward to the eighteenth century and start exploring the Georgian part. I'll warn you, there's a lot of it. I think we'll stick to the ground and first floors today. The second floor is largely empty and the attics have been untouched for years.'

'Attics?' A frisson of excitement shivered through her. As a child she had adored roaming through the attics at home, exploring chests filled with family treasures. Only there was nothing to discover in the recently renovated, perfectly decorated house. Photos sorted into date order? Yes. Tiaras dripping with diamonds or secret love letters? No. But here, in a house that epitomised history, she could find anything.

'Would you mind if one day I had a look? In the attics?'

Seb walked towards the door and stopped, his hand on the huge iron bolt. 'One day? I think you'll need to put aside at least six months. My family were hoarders—I would love to catalogue it all, although I suspect much of it is junk, but there's too much to do elsewhere. The whole house could do with some updating. I don't know if your talents run in that direction but please, feel free to make any changes you want. As long as they're in keeping with a grade one listed building,' he added quickly.

'And there I was, thinking I could paint the whole outside pink and add a concrete extension.' But she was strangely cheered. A house with twenty bedrooms and as many reception rooms— if you included the various billiard rooms, studies and galleries—was no small project. But taking it in hand gave her a purpose, a role here. Maybe, just maybe, she could make Hawksley Castle into a home. Into her home.

CHAPTER FIVE

'MORNING. HUNGRY?'

Seb half turned as Daisy slipped into the kitchen, tiptoeing as if she didn't want to offend him with her presence.

'Starving. I keep waiting for the nausea to start.' She was almost apologetic, as if he would accuse her of being a fraud if she wasn't doubled over with sickness. It would be easier, he admitted, if she were ill. He was after all taking it on trust that she was even pregnant in the first place, although she had offered him plenty of chances to wait for confirmation.

'You may be lucky and escape it altogether. How did you sleep?'

'Good, thanks. Turns out five-hundred-year-old beds are surprisingly comfy.'

The problem of where to put Daisy had haunted him since she had agreed to move in. To make this work, to fulfil her criteria as far as he could, meant he couldn't treat her like a guest and yet he wasn't ready to share his space with anyone.

Even though part of him couldn't help wondering what it would be like lying next to those long, silky limbs.

Luckily Georgian houses were built with this kind of dilemma in mind. When he first took a leave of absence and returned to Hawksley six months ago to try and untangle the complicated mess his father had left, he'd moved into his grandparents' old rooms, not his own boyhood bedroom on the second floor.

There was a suite adjoining, the old countess' suite, a throwback to not so long ago when the married couple weren't expected to regularly share a bed, a room or a bathroom. The large bedroom, small study, dressing room and bathroom occupied a corner at the back of the house with views over the lake to the woods and fields beyond. The suite was rather faded, last decorated some time around the middle of the previous century and filled with furniture of much older heritage but charming for all that.

'There is a door here,' he had said, showing her a small door discreetly set into the wall near the bed. 'It leads into my room. You can lock it if you would rather, but I don't bother.'

The words had hung in the air. Were they an invitation? A warning? He wasn't entirely sure.

It was odd, he had never really noticed the door before yet last night it had loomed in his eyeline, the unwanted focal point of his own room. He had known she was on the other side, just one turn of the handle away. Seb's jaw tightened as he flipped the bacon. He could visualise it now as if it were set before him. Small, wooden, nondescript.

'Did you lock the door?'

'Bolted it.'

'Good, wouldn't want the ghost of a regency rake surprising you in the middle of the night.'

Daisy wandered over to the kettle and filled it. Such a normal everyday thing to do—and yet such a big step at the same time. 'I'm sure bolts are no barrier to any decent ghosts, not rakish-type ones anyway. Coffee?'

'All set, thanks.' He nodded at the large mug at his elbow. The scene was very domestic in a formal, polite kind of way.

Daisy sniffed the several herbal teas she had brought with her and pulled a face. 'I miss coffee. I don't mind giving up alcohol and I hate blue cheese anyway but waking up without a skinny latte is a cruel and unusual punishment.'

'We could get some decaf.' Seb grabbed two plates and spooned the eggs and bacon onto them.

'I think you're missing the whole point of coffee. I'll give liquorice a try.' She made the hot drink and carried the mug over to the table, eying up the heaped plate of food with much greater enthusiasm. 'This looks great, thanks.'

'I thought we might need sustenance for the day ahead. Registrar at ten and I booked you into the doctor's here for eleven. I hope that's okay. And then we'd better let the staff and volunteers know our news, begin to make some plans.'

'Fine.' A loud peal rang through the house causing a slight vibration, and Daisy jumped, the eggs piled up on her fork tumbling back onto the plate. 'What on earth is that?'

Seb pushed his chair back and tried not to look too longingly at his uneaten breakfast. It was a long way from the kitchen to the door, plenty of time for his breakfast to cool. 'Doorbell. It's a little dramatic admittedly but the house is so big it's the only way to know if there's a visitor—and it's less obtrusive than a butler. Cheaper too.'

'Is it the gorgon? If I get turned to stone I expect you to rescue me.'

He tried not to let his mouth quirk at the apt nickname. There was definitely a heart of gold buried deep somewhere underneath Mrs Suffolk's chilly exterior but it took a long time to find and appreciate it. 'The volunteers have a key for the back door—there's only two working doors between the offices and the main house and I lock them both at night.'

'Good to know. I don't fancy being petrified in my bed.' Her words floated after him as he exited the kitchen and headed towards the front of the house.

Once, of course, the kitchen would have been part of the servants' quarters; it was still set discreetly behind a baize door, connected to the offices through a short passageway and one of the lockable doors that defined the partition between his personal space and the work space. But even his oh-so-formal grandparents had dispensed with live-in servants during the nineties and started to use the old kitchen themselves. For supper and breakfast at least.

His parents had brought their servants with them during the four years they had mismanaged

Hawksley. Not that they had ever stayed at the castle for longer than a week.

The doorbell pealed again, the deep tone melodic.

'On my way.' Seb pulled back the three bolts and twisted the giant iron key, making a mental note to oil the creaking lock. He swung open the giant door to be confronted with the sight of his future mother-in-law, a huge and ominously full bag thrown over one shoulder, a newspaper in one hand and a bottle of champagne in the other.

Seb blinked. Then blinked again.

'Goodness, Seb, you look like you've seen a ghost.' She thrust the champagne and the newspaper at him, muttering cryptically, 'Page five, darling. Where is Daisy?'

'Good morning, Mrs Huntingdon…'

'Sherry.' She swept past him. '"Mrs" makes me feel so old. And we are going to be family after all.'

Family. Not something he knew huge amounts about but he was pretty sure the tall, glamorous woman opposite wasn't a typical mother-in-law. 'Right, yes. This way. She's just eating breakfast.'

He led the supermodel through the hallway, wincing as he noticed her assess every dusty cornice, every scrap of peeling paper. 'My grandparents rather let the place go.'

'It's like a museum. Apt for you in your job, I suppose.' It didn't sound like a compliment.

They reached the kitchen and Sherry swept by him to enfold a startled-looking Daisy in her arms. 'Bacon? Oh, Daisy darling, the chances of you fitting sample sizes were small anyway but you'll never do it if you eat fried food. No, none for me, thank you. I don't eat breakfast.'

'Mum? What are you doing here?'

Seb couldn't help smiling at Daisy's face. She looked exactly as he felt: surprise mixed with wariness and shock.

'Darling, we have a wedding to plan and no time at all. Where else would I be? Now hurry up and eat that. We'll get you some nice fruit while we're out. Page five, Seb.'

Seb glanced down at the tabloid newspaper Sherry had handed him and opened it slowly, his heart hammering. Surely not, not yet…

He dropped it on the table, a huge picture of Daisy and himself smiling up from the smudged newsprint. 'Hot Prof Earl and Wild Child to Wed' screamed the headline. He stepped back, horror churning in the pit of his stomach, his hands clammy.

'I knew it.' Daisy's outraged voice cut into his stupor. 'They mentioned the expulsion. Why not my first in photography or my successful business?'

'I expect they also mentioned my parents' divorces, remarriages, drinking, drug taking and untimely deaths.' He knew he sounded cold, bitter and inhaled, trying to calm the inner tumult.

'Yes.' Her voice sounded small and Seb breathed in again, trying to calm the swirling anger. It wasn't her fault.

Although if she wasn't who she was then would they be so interested?

'I'm sorry,' she added and he swallowed hard, forcing himself to lay a hand upon her shoulder.

'Don't be silly, Daisy, of course they're interested. Seb is just as big a draw as you, more so probably.' Sherry's blue eyes were sharp, assessing.

'Yes,' he agreed tonelessly. 'We knew there would be publicity. I just thought we would have more time.'

If Daisy hadn't gone to Huntingdon Hall, hadn't involved her parents...

'The best thing to do is ignore it. Come along, darling. Show me the wedding venue. I don't have all day.'

Daisy sat for a moment, her head still bowed, cheeks pale. 'We have appointments at ten, Mum, so I only have half an hour. If you'd warned us you were coming I could have told you this morning was already booked up.'

'You two head off, I'll be fine here. There's plenty to do, just show me the venue.'

'Honestly, Mum. I can organise this quite easily. I really don't need you to do it.' There was a hint of desperation in Daisy's voice as she attempted to reason with her mother.

'I know very well that you prefer to do everything alone, Daisy. You make that quite clear.'

Daisy pushed her half-eaten breakfast away and, with an apologetic glance at Seb, took her mother's arm. 'Okay, you win. Seb, I put your breakfast back in the pan to keep warm. Come along, Mother. I don't think even you can fault the Tudor Hall.'

Seb watched them go before sliding his gaze back to the open newspaper. He focused on the picture. He was driving and Daisy was looking back, smiling. It must have been snapped as they left the hall. How hadn't he noticed the photographer?

Was this how their lives would be from now on? Every step, every conversation, every outing watched, scrutinised and reported on.

With one vicious movement he grabbed the paper and tore the article from it, screwing it into a ball and dropping it in the bin, his breath coming in fast pants. He wouldn't, couldn't be hounded. Cameras trained on him, crowds waiting outside the gate, microphones thrust into his face. He had been five the first time, as motorcycles and cars chased them down the country lanes.

His father had driven faster, recklessly. His mother had laughed.

The tantalising aroma of cooking bacon wafted through the air, breaking into his thoughts. Seb walked over to the stove, his movements slow and stiff. The frying pan was covered, the heat set to low and inside, warmed through to perfection, was his breakfast. Saved, put aside and kept for him.

When was the last time someone had done something, anything for him that they weren't paid to do?

It was just some breakfast, food he had actually

cooked, put aside. So why did his chest ache as he spooned it back onto his plate?

Daisy had to work hard to stop from laughing at the look on Seb's face. He stood in the Great Hall, staring about him as if he had been kidnapped by aliens and transported to an alternate universe.

And in some ways, he had.

Her mother had wasted no time in making herself at home, somehow rounding up two bemused if bedazzled volunteers to help her set up office in the Great Hall. Three tables in a U-shape and several chairs were flanked by a white board and a pin board on trestles with several sticky notes already attached to each. A seamstress's dummy stood to attention behind the biggest chair, a wreath of flowers on its head.

A carafe of water, a glass and a vase of flowers had been procured from somewhere and set upon the table and Sherry had proceeded to empty her huge bag in a Mary Poppins manner setting out two phones, a lever arch file already divided into labelled sections, a stack of wedding magazines and—Daisy groaned in horror—her own scrapbooks and what looked like her own Pinterest mood boards printed out and laminated.

So she planned weddings online? She was a wedding photographer! It was her job to get ideas and inspiration.

If Sherry Huntingdon ever turned her formidable mind towards something other than fashion then who knew what she'd achieve? World peace? An end to poverty? Daisy winced. That wasn't entirely fair; both her parents did a huge amount for charity, most of it anonymously. The Benefit Concert might be the most high-profile event but it was just the tip of the iceberg.

'There you are, Seb.' Sherry was pacing around the Great Hall, looking at the panelling and the other period details with approval. 'Before you whisk Daisy away I need a bit of information.'

'Whatever you need.' His eyes flickered towards the arsenal of paper, pens and planning materials set out with precision on the tables and a muscle began to beat in his stubbled jaw as his hands slowly clenched. 'Good to see that you've made yourself at home.'

'I think it's helpful to be right in the centre of things,' Sherry agreed, missing—or ignoring— his sarcastic undertone. 'Your nice man on the gate tells me that there are weddings booked in both weekends so I can't leave everything set up but we'll have the hall to ourselves for the four days before the wedding so I can make sure everything is perfect.'

Daisy noticed Seb's tense stance, the rigidity in his shoulders, and interrupted. 'It won't take four days to set up for a few family and friends—and it's such short notice I'm sure most people will have plans already.'

'Don't be ridiculous, of course they'll come. It'll be the wedding of the year—rock aristocracy to real aristocracy? They'll cancel whatever other plans they have, you mark my words. Now, the nice young man tells me the hall will seat two hundred so I'll need your list as soon as possible, Seb.'

'List?' The muscle was still beating. Daisy couldn't take her eyes off it. She wanted to walk over there, lay a hand on the tense shoulder and soothe the stress out of it, run a hand across his firm jawline and kiss the muscle into quiet acquiescence. She curled her fingers into her palms, allowing her nails to bite into her flesh, the sharp sting reminding her not to cross the line. To remain businesslike.

'I already did you a list, Daisy.' Of course she had. Numbly Daisy took the sheet of neatly typed names her mother handed her and scanned it expecting to see the usual mixture of relatives, her parents' friends and business associates and the group of people her age that her parents liked to socialise with: a few actors, singers and other cool, media-friendly twenty-somethings she had absolutely nothing in common with.

And yet…Daisy swallowed, heat burning the backs of her eyes. The names she read through rapidly blurring eyes were exactly—almost exactly—those she would have written herself. It was like a *This Is Your Life* recap: school friends, college friends, work associates, London friends plus of course the usual relatives and some of the older villagers, people she had known her entire life.

'This is perfect. How did you know?' Blinking furiously, Daisy forced back the threatening tears; all her life she had felt like the odd one out, the funny little addition at the end of the family, more a pampered plaything than a card-carrying, fully paid-up adult member of the family, a person who really mattered.

A person who they knew, who they understood. Maybe they understood her better than she had ever realised.

'Vi helped me.' Her mother's voice was a little gruff and there was a telltale sheen in her eyes. 'Is it right?'

'Almost perfect.' There were just a few amendments. Daisy swiftly added several new names, recent friends her family had yet to meet.

Seb moved, just a small rustle but enough to bring her back to the present, to the reality that was this wedding. What was she thinking?

Her hand shook a little bit as she reread the top lines. These were exactly the people she would want to share her wedding day with. Only…

'The thing is we did agree on a small wedding.' She tried to keep all emotion out of her voice, not wanting her mother to hear her disappointment or Seb to feel cornered. 'If we invited all these it would be a huge affair. I'll take a look at it and single out the most important friends. What do you think? Immediate family and maybe five extra guests each?' She looked around at the long hall, the vast timbered ceiling rearing overhead. They would rattle around in here like a Chihuahua in a Great Dane's pen.

But it was still a substantially larger affair than Seb wanted. Daisy allowed the piece of paper to float down onto the desk as if the thought of striking out the majority of the names didn't make her throat tighten.

Seb had moved, so silently she hadn't noticed, reaching over her shoulder to deftly catch the paper mid-fall. 'The problem is I don't actually have any immediate family.'

Daisy automatically opened her mouth to say something inane, something to smooth over the chasm his words opened up. Then she closed it again. What good were platitudes? But understanding shivered over her. No wonder this marriage was important to him. The baby was more than a potential heir; it would be all that he had. Responsibility crushed down on her. She had been so naïve, so happy at the thought of having a person in her life who needed her, depended on her. But the baby wasn't just hers. It was theirs.

'There are school friends.' He was scribbling away on the back of the list, his handwriting sure and firm. 'Other academics, publishing colleagues, staff and volunteers here and villagers I have known all my life. I think I will need eighty places including the plus ones but, if you agree, I propose a hog roast in a marquee in the courtyard in the evening and invite the whole village. Noblesse oblige I know but it's a tied village and expected.'

'Do you have a marquee?' Thank goodness her mother was on the ball because Daisy couldn't have spoken if her life had depended on it. He didn't want this, she knew that. People, publicity, fuss, photos and the inevitable press. The only answer, the only possible reason was that he was doing this for her.

She slipped her hand into his without thought or plan and his fingers curled around hers.

Maybe, just maybe this could work after all.

'Weddings here are all run and catered for by The Blue Boar, that's the village pub, and yes, they have several marquees of all sizes. Paul—' he smiled slightly, that devastating half-lift of his mouth '—the helpful man on the gate, he can give you all the details you need.'

'That is wonderful.' Her mother was rapidly taking notes. 'That gives me a lot to be getting on with. Rose will be doing the rings of course and Violet the flowers. You know what, Daisy, I think somehow we are going to be able to pull this wedding off.'

'We're going all the way into London?'

When she had left the day before Daisy had felt, fully aware of her own inner melodrama, as if she were being taken away from her beloved city for ever even though she knew full well that she would be returning for a studio shoot later that week. But it still felt slightly anticlimactic to be returning just over twenty-four hours later.

Her mother looked mildly surprised. 'Of course, we have a wedding dress to buy.' Her voice grew wistful. 'It was such a shame that Seb vetoed a Tudor theme. I think he would have carried off a doublet really well. And such an eminent historian, you would have thought he would have jumped at the chance to really live in the past.'

'So short-sighted.' Daisy couldn't suppress the gurgle of laughter that bubbled up as she remembered the utter horror on Seb's face when her mother had greeted them with her brilliant idea. 'I would have preferred regency though.'

'The building is all wrong but you were made to wear one of those high-waisted gowns. And breeches are possibly even better than doublet and hose.'

'Infinitely better.' Daisy settled herself into a more comfortable position, allowing her hand to move softly across her abdomen. All had been confirmed. She was definitely pregnant, close to seven weeks. Just as she had expected but it had been a relief to hear another human say it out loud.

A relief to give Seb the definitive tidings; backing out of the wedding now would have been awkward for both of them. It wasn't that she was actually beginning to enjoy the planning process, enjoy having her mother's undivided attention or even enjoy seeing Seb pulled so far out of his comfort zone he could barely formulate a sentence.

Except when the Tudor theme was mooted. He had been more than able to turn that idea down flat.

Once she had established where they were going Daisy took little notice of the route. It wasn't often she spent time alone with her mother.

Maybe if she had allowed her mother in a little more then there would have been more occasions like this but the price had always seemed too high. Her mother did have a tendency to try and take over, the wedding a perfect case in point.

But it came from a place of love; maybe she should have respected that more.

Daisy leant across and kissed her mother's still smooth and unlined cheek.

'Thank you,' she said. 'For helping.' It almost

hurt, saying the words, but she felt a sense of relief when they were out, as if she had been holding onto them for a long, long time.

Her mother's blue eyes widened. 'Of course I want to help. My baby, getting married. And there is so much to do. Hawksley may be grand but I've seen more up-to-date ruins.'

'Part of it is ruined.' Daisy was surprised at how protective she felt towards the stately building.

Her mother gave her a wry glance. 'I mean the house part. Really, darling, it's a major project. Some of the rooms have been untouched for years.'

'I just wish you had checked with Seb before organising the cleaners.' Only her mother could get an army of cleaners, decorators and handymen organised in under two hours. It had been a shock to arrive back from their morning appointments to find the car park full of various trade vans, the house overrun by ladders, buckets and pine scents.

'Most of the family will be staying in the house after all. Updating and decorating are your preserve, darling, but cleaning and touching up before the big day is very much mine. Consider it my wedding present to you both.'

Daisy tried not to sigh. Seb employed one cleaner who was responsible for the offices as well as the house and she barely made a dent in the few areas he used. It would be nice to see the main house brought up to hygienic standards: the paintwork fresh, the wood polished and the sash windows gleaming. At the same time it was so typical of her mother to wave her magic wand with extravagant generosity, to think that money would solve the problem regardless of how it made the recipients feel.

There had been a bleak look on Seb's face when he surveyed the workers. He had withdrawn into his study pleading work and Daisy hadn't felt able to follow him in there.

The car drew up outside the iconic golden stone building that housed Rafferty's, London's premier designer store.

'It's simply too late for a gown to be made for you. I am owed a lot of favours but even I can't work miracles. But then I remembered what a fabulous collection Nina keeps here at Rafferty's. She has promised that she can have any gown altered to fit you in the timescale. Luckily I had my pick of the new spring/summer collections in Fashion Week last year so there will be something suitable for me.' Her mother sounded vaguely put upon, as if she were being expected to put an outfit together from a duster and an old feather boa, not premier one of the several haute couture outfits that had been made specifically for her.

Daisy felt the old shiver of excitement as they exited the car and walked into the famous domed entrance hall. It was once said you could buy anything and become anybody at Rafferty's—as long as you had the money. Would she become the bride of her dreams?

They were met at the door and whisked upstairs to the bridal department, an impressive gallery decorated in Rafferty's distinctive art deco style. The entrance to the department, reached through an archway, was open to the public and sold an array of bridal accessories including lingerie, shoes, tiaras and some ready-to-wear bride and bridesmaids dresses. But it was the room beyond, tactfully hidden behind a second, curtained arch, where the real magic lay. This room was accessed by appointment only. Today, Daisy and her mother were the only customers.

It needed little decoration and the walls were painted a warm blush white, the floor a polished mahogany. The sparkle and glamour came from the dresses themselves; every conceivable length, every shade of white from ice through to deep cream, a few richer colours dotted around: a daring red, rich gold, vibrant silver, pinks and rich brocades.

Daisy was glad of the cosy-looking love seats and chaises scattered about. So much choice was making her head whirl.

'Champagne?' Nina, the department manager who had been dressing the city's brides for nearly forty years, came over with a bottle of Dom Perignon, chilled and opened.

'No, thanks.' Daisy thought rapidly. 'I want a clear head. There's so much choice.'

'A large glass for me, please.' Violet walked in, slightly out of breath. 'I sense it's going to be a long afternoon. Rose says hi, don't make her wear frills and definitely not shiny satin.'

'They're all so beautiful.' Their mother was already halfway down a glass of champagne, a wistful look in her eyes as she fingered the heavy silks, slippery satins and intricate laces. 'Obviously I wouldn't have changed my wedding to your father for the world. It was very romantic, just us, in a tiny chapel. I was barefoot with flowers in my hair. But I did miss out on all this...'

Her gaze encompassed the room. 'Which is why, Daisy darling, I am determined that no matter how whirlwind your wedding, no matter how little time we have, you are going to have the day you always dreamed of.'

CHAPTER SIX

'YOU LOOK TERRIBLE. What's wrong?'

Daisy, Seb had discovered in the week they had been living together, was just like him—an early bird. She usually appeared in the kitchen just a few moments after he did, already dressed, ready to moan about the lack of caffeine in her day while hopefully trying yet another of the seemingly endless array of herbal teas she had brought with her, hoping to discover the one to replace her beloved lattes.

Today she was dressed as usual, if a little more demure, in a grey skater-style dress with an embroidered yellow hem, a yellow knitted cap pulled back over her head. But there was no exaggerated groaning when she saw his coffee, no diving on the toast as if she hadn't eaten in at least a month. Instead she pulled out a chair and collapsed into it with a moan.

'Why, why, why did I agree to start work at nine?' She looked at the clock on the wall and slid further down her seat. 'It's going to take me well over an hour to get there. I'll need to set off in ten minutes.'

'Toast?' Seb pushed the plate towards her but she pushed it back with an exaggerated shudder.

'No, it's far too early for food.'

She hadn't said that yesterday at a very similar time. Between them they had demolished an entire loaf of bread.

'Is that a new brand of coffee?' Daisy was looking at his cup of coffee as if he had filled it with slurry from the cow sheds, her nose wrinkled in disgust.

'Nope, the usual.'

'It smells vile.'

Seb took another look. She was unusually pale, the violet shadows under her eyes pronounced despite powder, the bright lipstick a startling contrast to her pallor. 'Didn't you sleep well?'

'I could have slept for ever.' She sniffed again and went even paler. 'Are you sure that's the usual brand? Have you made it extra strong?' She pressed her hand to her stomach and winced.

'You look really ill. I think you should go back to bed.'

'I can't.' The wail was plaintive. 'I have a wedding to photograph. I'm due at the bride's house at nine for the family breakfast followed by the arrival of the bridesmaids and getting ready. I need to be at the groom's at half eleven for best man and ushers then back to the bride's for final departures, church at one and then the reception.'

'With a blog up by midnight and the first pictures available the next day?' His mouth folded into a thin line. It was a ridiculous schedule.

'That's what they pay me for.'

'There is no way you are going to be able to manage an eighteen-hour day on no breakfast.'

Daisy pushed her chair back and swayed, putting a hand onto the table to steady herself. 'I don't have any choice. I work for myself, Seb. I can't just call in sick. Besides, I'm not ill, I'm pregnant. This is self-inflicted, like a hangover. I just have to deal with it.'

'It's nothing like a hangover.' He stopped as she winced, a hand to her head. 'You need an assistant.'

'Possibly, but unless you can produce one out of one of the trunks in the attic that's not going to help with today.'

Seb regarded her helplessly. He wanted to march her back upstairs, tuck her in and make her soup.

He was responsible for the slight green tinge to her skin and the shadows under her eyes.

But she was right, if she cried off a wedding on the day her reputation would be shattered. 'Can anyone cover for you?'

'Seb, this is morning sickness not a twenty-four-hour bug.' Her voice rose in exasperation. 'It could last for days, or weeks, or even months. What about Monday's engagement shoot? Or next Saturday's wedding? Or the baby photos on Wednesday? I can't just walk away from all my responsibilities.'

'No, but you can plan ahead.'

'But none of this *was* planned. Don't treat me like I'm some fluffy little girl without a brain cell.'

Woah, where had that come from?

'I didn't mean to offend you.' He knew he sounded stiff but this: histrionics, overreacting, unreasonable responses to reasonable points. It was everything he didn't want in his life.

To his surprise Daisy let out a huge sigh and slumped. 'I'm sorry, I am just so tired. You're right, I do need to start planning how I am going to cover my commitments over the next year.'

It was over, just like that. No escalation, no

screaming, no smashing of crockery. Just an apology.

'I could have phrased it better.' It wasn't as full an apology as hers but it was all he could manage in his shock.

'I have been meaning to talk to Sophie. She was on my course and specialises in portraits, personal commissions mostly although she's been beginning to get some magazine work. Her studio rent was just doubled and now I'm not living in mine I thought we might join forces and she could cover weddings for me in lieu of rent, or at least give me a hand. But that doesn't solve today.'

No. It didn't.

Daisy took one dragging step towards the door and then another. Her laptop case, camera case and tripod were neatly piled up, waiting. How she was going to carry them he had no idea.

And she really needed to eat something.

'I'll come with you and help.'

She half turned, the first flicker of a smile on her face. 'You? Do you know when to use a fifty-millimetre, an eighty-five-millimetre or switch to a wide-angled lens?'

'No, I can barely use the camera on my phone,'

Seb admitted. 'But I can fetch, carry, set up, organise groups, make sure you eat.'

A flicker of hope passed over her face. 'Don't you have a million and one things to do here?'

'Always.' Seb grimaced as he remembered the unfinished grant applications, the paperwork that seemed to grow bigger the more he did. Not to mention his real work, the research that seemed more and more impossible every day. The looming deadline for a book still in note form. 'Promise me you'll chat to Sophie tomorrow and at least sort out a willing apprentice for next week and I'll come and help.'

She was tempted, he could see. 'You really don't mind?'

'No, not at all. On the condition I drive and you try and eat something in the car.' The grant applications could wait, the paperwork could wait. He'd be worrying all day if he allowed her to walk out of the door and start a gruelling day on her feet without someone to watch out for her.

The sooner she got an assistant or partner, the better.

There were times when Seb wondered if all that sassy style and confidence was only skin deep.

When he thought he saw a flash of vulnerability in the blue eyes. But not here. Not today.

If Daisy still felt sick she was hiding it well. She was all quiet control and ease as she snapped: candid shots, posed shots, detailed close-ups. Always polite, always professional but in complete control, whether it was putting the nervy mother of the bride at her ease or settling the exuberant best man and ushers down enough to take a series of carefully choreographed shots.

She was everywhere and yet she was totally discreet. Focused on the job at hand. Seb followed her with bags and the box of ginger biscuits, completely out of place in this world of flowers and silks and tears.

Even the groom had had tears in his eyes as the bride had finally—an entire twenty minutes late—walked down the aisle.

As for the mother of the bride, five tissues hadn't been enough to staunch her sobs. The whole thing was a hysterical nightmare. Leaving the church had been a huge relief and he had gulped in air like a drowning man.

But the ordeal wasn't over.

'I don't understand what else there is for you to do.' Daisy had directed him towards a woodland nearby and Seb was following her down the chipping-strewn path. 'You must have taken at least three hundred pictures already. How many group shots outside the church? His family, her family, his friends, her friends, his colleagues, her colleagues. The neighbours, passers-by...'

'Far more than three hundred.' She threw him a mischievous smile. 'Bored?'

'It just takes so long. No photos at our wedding, Daisy. Not like this.'

'No.' The smile was gone. 'But ours is different. We don't need to document every moment.'

'Just the obvious ones.' Perversely he was annoyed she wasn't trying to talk him round. 'It would seem odd otherwise.'

'If you want.' She chewed her bottom lip as she looked at him thoughtfully. 'I think I'm going to change the order a little bit as you are here. If I put you in charge of the photo booth then there is some entertainment for the guests while I do the couple's portraits in the woods. Is that okay?'

Seb blinked. He was here to carry bags, not perform. 'The what? Do I have to do anything?'

'Smile. Tell them to say cheese. Press a button, four times. Can you manage that?'

Possibly. 'What do you mean by photo booth? Like a passport photo? At a wedding?'

She shot him an amused look. 'In a way, you know, teenagers sit in a photo booth and take silly pictures—or at least they did before selfies became ubiquitous.'

He shook his head. 'No, never did it. I've never taken a selfie either.'

Her mouth tilted into a smile. 'That doesn't surprise me. But you know what I mean? This is the same, only with props. And not a booth, just me with a camera—or in this case you. They put on silly accessories and then stand in front of a frame and try different poses. I print them up as a long strip of four pictures.'

Seb stared at her incredulously. 'Why on earth do you do that?'

'Because it's fun.' She rolled her eyes at him. 'I'll set the tripod up. All you need to do is explain they have three seconds to change pose and press the button. Honestly, Seb, it's fine. A monkey could do it.'

'And where will you be?'

'Portrait time. Followed by more group shots. And then candid evening and reception shots. Having fun yet?'

'Absolutely. The thought of wandering around these woods for hours carrying your cases is my idea of a perfect day. Sure you know where you're going?' They seemed to be going further into the woodland with no building in sight.

'Yep, I did the engagement shoot here. Ah, here we go.' She stopped, a hand to her mouth. 'Oh, Seb. Look at it. Isn't it utterly perfect?'

Seb came to a halt and stared. Where was the hotel? Or barn? A barn would be nice and cosy. Cosier than open canvas at least. 'They must be crazy? An outdoor wedding in April?'

'It's not outdoors!'

'It's in a tent.'

'It's a tepee.'

'You say tent, I say tepee.'

Daisy ignored him as he hummed the words, a chill running through him as the next line of the song ran through his head.

There was no calling the whole thing off now, not easily. It had escalated far beyond his wildest imaginings: a guest list of over two hundred not including the evening guests, dresses, button holes, hog roasts, centrepieces, cravats—Sherry's determination and vision taking it to a level neither Seb nor Daisy had wanted or sanctioned.

Did he want to call it off? He still wanted to marry Daisy; it was still the most sensible solution. But this circus his life was becoming was out of control. His peaceful Oxford existence seemed further and further away.

Although that wasn't Daisy's fault. Running Hawksley was more than a full-time job and not one he was finding it easy to delegate no matter how much he missed his old life.

'Oh, that's perfect.' Daisy's voice broke in on his thoughts and he pushed them to one side. He couldn't change anything—including the wedding. He owed her that much.

Daisy was lost in a world of her own. It was fascinating to watch her pace, focus, move again as she looked at the scene before her, crouching down to check angles and squinting against the light. No insouciance, no hesitation, just quietly in control.

Seb moved with her, trying to see with her, picture what she pictured. The path opened out into a woodland glade, which had been decorated with cheerful bunting and swaying glass lanterns. In the middle of the glade the huge canvas tepee stood opened up on three sides to the elements—

although Daisy promised there were covers ready to be fastened on if April proved true to its name and christened the wedding with showers.

A wooden floor had been laid and trestle tables and benches ran down the sides, the middle left bare for dancing. A stage held the tables covered with food for the buffet; later food would be switched for the band. Two smaller tents were pitched to one side, one holding the bar and the other a chill-out area complete with beanbags.

On the other side a gazebo was pitched, the table inside heaped with a variety of wigs, hats, waistcoats and other props. A large frame hung from the tree beside it. This was to be Seb's workspace for his first—and hopefully last—foray into professional photography.

He had never been to a wedding like this before and something about its raw honesty unsettled him; it was a little Bohemian, a touch homespun with its carefully carefree vibe.

'Look at these colours. Their friends and family supplied the food in lieu of presents. Don't you think that's lovely? Everyone made something.' Daisy was over at the buffet table, camera out, focusing on a rich-looking salad of vibrant green leaves, red pomegranate seeds and juicy oranges.

'It depends on their cooking skills.' If Seb asked his friends and colleagues to bring a dish they would buy something from a local deli, not spend time and love creating it themselves. He looked at a plate of slightly lumpy cakes, the icing uneven, and a hollow feeling opened up in his chest.

Someone had lavished care and attention on those cakes, making up with enthusiasm for what they lacked in skill. That was worth more than clicking on an item on a wedding list or writing a cheque.

Daisy looked up at a rustle and relaxed again as a bird rose out of a tree. 'Tell me as soon as you hear anybody. I want to capture their faces as they walk in.' The guests were being brought to the woodland by coach via a drinks reception at the local pub, the place where the bride and groom had first met.

'Shouldn't you be sitting down and maybe eating something while there's a lull?' But she didn't hear him, lost in a world of her own.

'Look, Seb,' she said softly, and he did, trying to see what she saw as she zoomed in on the brightly patterned bunting that bedecked the inside of the tent as well as the glade.

'These are the touches that make this wedding so special. Did you know that Ella and her friends made the bunting during her hen party? And look at these.' The camera moved to focus in on one of the paintings propped up on the small easels that were the centrepiece on each table. 'Rufus painted these, a different tree for each table—oak, laurel, ash, apple, all native species. Aren't they gorgeous?'

Studying one of the confident line drawings, Seb had to admit that they were. 'He's very talented.'

'Even the wedding favours are home-made. Ella spent her first day off work making the fudge, and her gran embroidered the bags. Look, they all have a name on. One for each guest.'

'It must have taken months.' Seb kept pace with her as she wandered.

'It did. This wedding is a real labour of love. Even the venue belongs to one of their friends.'

The contrast with their impending nuptials couldn't be starker.

But theirs wasn't a labour of love. It was a convenient compromise. Mutually beneficial. Maybe it was better to have the glitz and the glamour so lovingly lavished upon them by Sherry Huntingdon. Anything as heartfelt as this wedding, any one of the myriad tiny, loving, personal touches would be completely out of place at his wedding. Would be a lie.

'Admit it, you had fun.' Daisy threw herself into her favourite rocking chair, grateful for the warmth and the cushion supporting her aching back. She crooned to Monty as he padded over to lay his head in her lap. He was already her most faithful friend much to Seb's much-voiced disgust, possibly because she was not averse to sneaking him titbits from her plate.

'I'm not sure fun is the right word.' Seb filled the kettle and stifled a yawn. 'I always said your schedule was crazy but it's more than that, it's downright gruelling.' But there was respect in his voice and it warmed her. She was well aware of his opinion about her job.

And he was right, it *was* gruelling, somehow even more so in a small intimate setting like today's woodland scene. Gruelling and odd, being part of someone's wedding, integral to it and yet not connected. A stranger. As the afternoon faded to evening and the guests drank more, ate more, danced and the mood shifted into party atmosphere the gap between the help and the guests widened. There were times it was almost voyeuristic watching the interactions from the sidelines. It had been nice to have company today.

She really should get an assistant and not just because of her pregnancy.

'I would normally be the first to suggest you rest but don't you have a blog to write? If it's not up before midnight the world shifts on its axis and Cupid dies?' He held up a ginger teabag for her approval. Daisy considered it without enthusiasm before pulling a face and agreeing.

She shifted in the chair, pulling her feet under her, and began to pull at Monty's long, soft ears. He gave a small throaty groan and moved closer. 'Did it in the car. It's amazing, home before midnight and job done, for today at least.'

She looked over at her bag, the cameras loaded with images. 'Tomorrow however is most definitely another day. I promised them thirty images before they go away on honeymoon. Still, I feel much better than I thought I would. I don't suppose you would consider a permanent career as bag carrier and chauffeur—and photo-booth operator?' She smiled, a sly note creeping into her voice. 'You were quite a hit. Some of the women went back to have their photo taken again and again.'

'How do you know? I still can't believe it took an hour and a half to take those woodland shots. I think you went for a nap somewhere leaving me to do all the work.'

'Oh, I was. Curled up in a pile of leaves like Hansel and Gretel while woodland birds sang me to sleep and squirrels brought me nuts. And I know because the sexy photographer was quite the topic of conversation—and I don't think they meant me!'

'Jealous?'

Daisy didn't answer for a moment, focusing all her attention on Monty as she scratched behind his ears, the spaniel leaning against her blissfully. 'A little, actually.' She still couldn't look at him as she chose her next words carefully. 'There was a little bit of me that wanted to tell them that you weren't available, that you were mine.' She looked up.

Seb froze, his eyes fixed on her.

The blood was pounding hard in her ears, like a river in full flood. What had she said that for?

Not even married and already she was pushing too hard, wanting too much. 'Which is silly because you're not,' she back-pedalled, desperately wanting to make light of the words. 'Maybe it's pregnancy hormones not wanting my baby's hunter gatherer to shack up in someone else's cave.' She made herself hold his gaze, made herself smile although it felt unnatural.

'I have no intention of shacking up in anyone's cave.' She winced at the horror in his voice and his face softened. 'I promised you, Daisy, I promised you that if you married me I would be in this completely.' He paused and she held her breath, waiting for the inevitable caveat. 'As much as I can be.' There it was. Known, expected. Yet it still hurt.

And she didn't want to dwell on why. Maybe she was beginning to believe their fantasy a little too much, fool that she was.

'But there will be nobody else, you have no reason to worry on that score.'

'Thank you.' She exhaled, a low painful breath. 'It's just difficult, the difference between the public and the private. I know I asked you to pretend but I admit I didn't realise it would be so hard.'

'Why?' He hadn't moved.

'Why what?'

'Why are we pretending? Why don't you want to be honest?'

Her eyes flickered back to Monty and she focused on the fuzzy top of his head, drawing each ear lovingly through her hands, trying to think of a way to explain that wouldn't make her sound too pathetic. 'It's a bit of a family joke, that I'm always falling in and out of love, that I'm a hopeless romantic. Even when I was a little girl I knew that I wanted to get married, to have children. But I wanted more than just settling down. I wanted what Mum and Dad have.'

'They're one in a million, Daisy.' Ouch, there it was. Pity.

'Maybe, but I know it's possible. It's not that they wouldn't understand us marrying for the baby, wouldn't be supportive. But they'd know I was giving up on my dream. I don't want to do that to them.' She paused then looked straight at him. 'As well as to myself.

'All my parents want is for me to be happy. They don't ask for anything more than that. When I was photographed and expelled they were disappointed, of course they were, although they didn't yell or punish me—but they weren't surprised either. They knew I'd mess up, somehow. And now I've messed up again. I was so determined to do it right, to show them I could cope on my own.'

'I think you are being hard on yourself—and on them,' he added unexpectedly. 'They adore you. Do you know how lucky you are to have that? People who care about you? Who only want you to be happy?'

All Daisy could do was stare at him in shock. 'I...' she began but he cut her off.

'I agree, lying to your family is wrong and I wish I had never agreed—but do you know what I fear? That you're right, that if you tell them the truth then they will stop you, they will show you that with a family like yours there is no way in hell you have to shackle yourself to me, that you and the baby will be fine, that you won't need me.'

'No, you're the baby's father and nothing will change that. Of course the baby will need you.' There was so much she didn't know, so much that she feared—but of this she was convinced.

She could need him too. If she allowed herself. Today had been almost perfect: help, support, wordless communication. But she knew it was a one-off. She had to train herself to enjoy these days when they came—and to never expect them.

'I hope so.' His smile was crooked. 'As for the rest, Daisy, you messed up at sixteen. Big deal. At least you learned from it, got on with your life, made something of yourself. You're not the only member of your family—or mine—to have dominated the headlines. Both your sisters spent their time on the front covers and they were older than you.'

'I know.' Could she admit it to him? The guilt she never allowed herself to articulate to anyone? Not even herself. 'But Violet was set up. Horribly and cruelly and callously set up and betrayed— and I don't think it is a coincidence that it wasn't long after everything that happened to me. I often wondered.' She paused. 'I think it was because of me. I had dropped out of the headlines so they went after my sister. And they destroyed her.'

'It's because of who your parents are, simple as that. You're all wealthy and beautiful.' A shiver went through her at the desire in his eyes as he said the last word. 'You're connected. People love that stuff. That's why we have to be careful, not a breath of scandal. Or they'll never leave us alone.'

Daisy knew how deadly publicity could be, had experienced the painful sting firsthand, watched one sister flee the country and the other hide herself away. Had done her best to stay under the parapet for the last eight years. But she didn't have the visceral fear Seb had.

He was right, they couldn't allow their child to grow up under the same cloud. Which meant she had to stick to their agreement. A civilised, businesslike, emotion-free marriage. She had to grow up.

'What are you thinking, Daisy?' His voice was low and the green eyes so dark they were almost black.

'That you're right. That I can do this.'

His mouth quirked into that devastating half smile and Daisy's breath hitched. 'Marriage is going to be a lot easier than I imagined if you're going to keep on thinking I'm right.'

Her chin tilted. 'This is a one-off, not carte blanche.'

His slow grin was a challenge. 'Just how right am I?'

'What do you mean?' But she knew. She knew by the way it was suddenly hard to get her breath. She knew by the way his voice had thickened. She knew by the way his eyes were fixed on hers. She knew by the heat swirling in her stomach, the anticipation fizzing along her skin.

She knew because they had been here before.

The memory of that night was impressed on each and every nerve ending and they heated up in anticipation, the knowledge of every kiss, every touch imprinted there, wanting, needing a replay.

'How in are you, Daisy?' His meaning was unmistakeable.

The heat was swirling round her entire body, a haze of need making it hard to think. They were going to get married, were going to raise a child, make a life together. They had every right to take that final step. Every need.

So he didn't love her? That hadn't mattered before, had it? A mutual attraction combined with champagne and the bittersweet comedown she always experienced after a wedding had been enough.

And it wasn't as if she were foolish enough to go falling in love with someone after just one week, someone who made it very, very clear that love was always going to be a step too far.

He didn't love her. But he wanted her. The rigidity of his pose, his hands curled into loose fists, the intensity of his gaze told her that. Every instinct told her that.

And, oh, she wanted him. She had tried to fight

it, hide it, but she did. The line of his jaw, the way he held his hands, the dark hair brushed carelessly back, the amused glint that lit up the green eyes and softened the austere features.

The way each accidental touch burned through her, every look shot through to her core.

And, dear God, his mouth. Her eyes moved there and lingered. Well cut, firm, capable. She wanted to lick her way along the jaw, kiss the pulse in his neck and move up to nibble her way along his lips. She wanted to taste him. For him to taste her. To consume her.

The heat intensified, burning as her breasts ached and the pull in her body made the distance, any distance unbearable.

There was nothing to stop her. They were going to be married. It was practically her right to touch him. To be touched.

It was definitely her right to kiss him.

And just because she had been fixated on romance in the past didn't mean she had to be in the future. After all, look how quickly she tumbled out of love, disillusioned and disappointed.

There was a lot to be said for a businesslike, respectful marriage. Especially marriage with benefits.

She swallowed, desperate for moisture.

'Daisy?' It was more of a command than a question and she was tired. Tired of fighting the attraction that burned between them, tired of being afraid to take it on.

She stood up, slowly, allowing her body to stretch out, knowing how his eyes lingered on her legs, up her body, rested on her breasts sharply outlined by her stretch. She saw him swallow.

'I'm going to bed,' she said, turning towards the door. She paused, looked back. 'Joining me?'

CHAPTER SEVEN

THE CUP TILTED as Seb nudged Daisy's door open and he hastily righted it before the lurid green mixture slopped onto the threadbare but valuable nineteenth-century runner. The tea was supposed to be completely natural but he'd never seen anything that resembled that particular green in nature.

He didn't wait for an answer but opened the door. 'Daisy? Tea.'

Luckily the nausea of last week had yet to grow into anything more debilitating but Daisy still found the first hour of the day difficult. A cup of something hot helped although replacing her beloved caffeine was still proving problematic. She was going to run out of new flavours of herbal tea to try soon.

'I'm in the bath.' A splashing sound proved her words.

'I'll just leave it here.' Seb tried to put the image of long, bubble-covered limbs and bare, wet torsos out of his mind as he placed the tea onto the small table by her window. He didn't have time for distractions, especially naked ones.

He turned and took in the bedroom properly. He hadn't set foot in here since Daisy had moved in two weeks ago. It had been the first suite tackled by her mother and, although the nineteen-fifties chintz flowery wallpaper still covered the walls, the furniture was still the heavy, stately mahogany and the carpet as threadbare as the landing's, the paintwork was fresh and white and the room smelled of a fresh mixture of beeswax, fresh air and Daisy's own light floral scent.

It wasn't just the aesthetic changes though. Daisy had somehow taken the room and made it hers from the scarves draped over the bedposts to the hat stand, commandeered from the hallway and now filled with a growing selection of her collection. Every time she went back to her studio she brought a few more. There were times when Seb feared the entire castle would be overtaken by hats.

Pictures of her parents and sisters were on one bedside table, a tower of stacked-up paperbacks on the second. A brief perusal showed an eclectic mix of nineteen-thirties detective novels, romances, two of last year's Booker Prize shortlist and a popular history book on Prince Rupert by one of Seb's colleagues and rivals.

Jealousy, as unwanted as it was sharp, shot through him. She did read history, just not his books it seemed.

'Get over yourself, Beresford,' he muttered, half amused, half alarmed by the instant reaction. It was professional jealousy sure, but still unwarranted. Unwanted.

A brief peek into the dressing room showed a similar colonisation. The dressing table bestrewn with pots and tubes, photos of herself and her sisters and friends he had yet to meet tucked into the mirror. The study was a little more austere, her laptop set up at the desk, her diary, open and filled with her scrawling handwriting, next to it.

Hawksley Castle had a new mistress.

Only the bed looked unrumpled. Daisy might bathe, dress and work in her rooms but she slept in his. Much as her nineteenth-century counterpart might have done she arrived in his bed cleansed, moisturised and already in the silky shorts and vest tops she liked to sleep in. Not a single personal item had migrated through the connecting door.

A buzz in his pocket signalled a message or a voicemail. It was almost impossible to get a decent mobile signal this side of the castle. Seb quite liked not being wired in twenty-four hours a day.

He pulled his phone out and listened to the message, wincing as he did so.

'Problems?' Daisy appeared at the bathroom door clad in nothing but a towel.

'My agent.' He stuffed the phone back into his pocket, glancing at Daisy as he did so.

He drew in a long, deep breath. It was impossible to ignore the twinge of desire evoked by her creamy shoulders, the outline of her body swathed in the long creamy towel.

The towels were another of Sherry's luxurious little additions to the house. By the date of the wedding Hawksley would resemble a five-star hotel more than a run-down if stately family home.

There were fresh flowers, renewed every other day, in all the repainted, cleaned bedrooms as well as in the bigger salons and hallways. Every bathroom, cloakroom and loo was ornamented with expensive soaps, hand creams and bath salts. In one way the luxurious touches hid the signs of elegant decay, but Seb couldn't help calculate how the price of the flowers alone could be better spent on plumbing, on the roof, on the myriad neglected maintenance jobs that multiplied daily.

No matter. Seb would give Sherry her head until the wedding but after that, no more. He wouldn't accept a penny, not even from his bride-to-be's indulgent and very wealthy parents. Hawksley was his inheritance, his responsibility, his burden.

'What did she want on a Saturday?' Daisy sat herself at her dressing table and began to brush out her hair. Seb's eyes followed the brush as it fought its way through the tangled locks leaving smooth tresses in its wake.

'Just to finalise arrangements for this afternoon.' And to try and start another conversation about a television deal. He would shut that down pretty fast although the numbers must be good to make her this persistent.

'This afternoon?'

'I'm lecturing. Didn't I mention it? Talking of which…' He looked at his watch, blinking as he caught the time. 'What are you still doing sat in a towel? Shouldn't you be capturing a bride's breakfast? Or is this one a late-rising bride?'

She shook her head, the newly brushed hair lifting with the movement. 'I have the whole weekend off. Sophie's covering today's wedding for me as a trial. They didn't have the full engagement-shot package so I don't have a personal relationship with them. It seemed like a good place for her to try and see how it works. I do have a few interviews tomorrow with possible assistants but today I am completely free.' She pulled a face. 'That can't be right, can it? Whatever will I do?'

Seb looked at her critically. She still looked drawn and tired. 'You could do with a day off. Between wedding planning and work you never seem to stop.'

'Says the man who put in sixteen hours on the estate yesterday and still wanted to do research when he came home.'

'Technically I am on a research year, not an estate management year.' The ever-present fear crowded in. Could he do both? What if he had to give up his professorship? Swap academia for farming? He pushed it aside. That was a worry for another day.

'Besides, I'm not turning greener than that drink of yours every morning and growing another human being. Why don't you book yourself into a spa or have a day shopping?'

She wrinkled her nose. 'Are those the only relaxing pursuits you can think of? I can't do most spa treatments and the last thing I want to do is shop, not after motherzilla of the bride's efforts.'

Sherry had been keeping Daisy hard at it. Seb had barely seen her all week. She was either holed up in the Great Hall creating wedding favours, shopping for last-minute essential details or back in her studio, working.

Things would be much easier if she had a studio here. Would she want that? Moving her hats across was one thing, moving her professional persona another. Seb adored his library but there were times when he missed his college rooms with an almost physical pain. The peace, the lack of responsibility beyond his work, his students,

'My lecture's in Oxford. I doubt that would be relaxing or interesting. But maybe you could walk around some of the colleges, have lunch there.' His eyes flickered over to the book by her bed. 'Or you could come to the lecture.'

The blurring of professional and private had to happen at some point.

'What's the lecture on?'

'The history of England as reflected in a house like Hawksley.' His mouth twisted. 'It's the subject of my next book, luckily. It's hard enough finding time to work as it is, at least I'm on site. It's a paid popular lecture so not too highbrow. You might enjoy it.'

He could have kicked himself as soon as he uttered the words. Her face was emotionless but her eyes clouded. 'Not too highbrow? So even dullards like me have a chance of understanding it?'

'Daisy, there's nothing dull about you. Will you come? I'll take you out for dinner afterwards.'

There it was, more blurring. But he had promised respect and friendship. That was all this was.

'Well, if there's food.' But her eyes were still clouded, her face gave nothing away. 'What time do you want to leave? I'll meet you downstairs.'

'What an incredible place. I've never looked around the colleges before.' Daisy focused the lens onto the green rectangle of lawn, the golden columns framing it like a picture.

'Maybe it's because I knew I had no chance of actually coming here.' She clicked and then again, capturing the sun slanting through the columns, lighting up the soft stone in an unearthly glow.

'But you wouldn't have wanted to come here. You went to one of the best art colleges in the country. I doubt that they would have even let me through the door.' Daisy bit back a giggle. She had seen Seb's attempts to draw just once, when he was trying to show Sherry how the marquee connected to the hall. It was good to know there were some areas where she had him beat.

'You could pretend you were creating some kind of post-modern deconstruction of the creative process.' She followed the quadrangle round with her viewfinder. 'This place is ridiculously photogenic. I bet it would make a superb backdrop for wedding photos.'

'It's always about weddings with you, isn't it?' Seb slid a curious glance her way and she tried to keep her face blank. His scrutiny unnerved her. He always made her feel so exposed, as if he could see beyond the lipstick and the hats, beyond the carefully chosen outfits. She hoped not. She wasn't entirely sure that there was any substance underneath her style.

'It's my job.' She kept her voice light. 'You must walk in here and see the history in each and every stone. It's no different.'

He was still studying her intently and she tried not to squirm, swinging the camera around to focus on him. 'Smile!'

But his expression didn't change. It was as if he

was trying to see through her, into the heart of her. She took a photo, and then another, playing with the focus and the light.

'Why photography? I would have thought you would have had enough of being on the other side of the lens?'

It was the million-dollar question. She lowered the camera and leant against one of the stone columns. Despite the sunlight dancing on it the stone was cold, the chill travelling through her dress. 'Truth is I didn't mind the attention as a kid,' she admitted, fiddling with her camera strap so she didn't have to look up and see judgement or pity in his eyes. 'We felt special. Mum and Dad were so adored, and there was no scandal, so all the publicity tended to be positive—glamorous red carpets at premieres or at-home photo shoots for charities. It wasn't until I was sixteen that I realised the press could bite as easily as it flattered.'

'Lucky you.' His voice was bleak. 'I was five when I was first bitten.'

She stole a look at him but his gaze was fixed unseeingly elsewhere. Poor little boy, a pawn in his parents' destructive lives. 'It was such a shock when it happened, seeing myself on the front pages. I felt so exposed. I know it wasn't clever.' She traced the brand name on her camera case, remembering, the need for freedom, the urge for excitement, the thrill of the illicit. 'But most sixteen-year-olds play hooky just once, try and get a drink underage somehow just once. They just don't do it under the public's condemning gaze.'

One set of photos, one drunken night, one kiss—the kind of intense kiss that only a sixteen-year-old falling in love could manage—and her reputation had been created, set in stone and destroyed.

'You couldn't have stuck to the local pub?'

He was so practical! She grinned, able to laugh at her youthful self now. 'Looking back, that was the flaw in my plan. But honestly, we were so naive we couldn't think where to go. The village landlord at home would have phoned Dad as soon as I stepped up to the bar. The pubs nearest school seemed to have some kind of convent schoolgirl sensor. We all knew there was no point trying there. Tana and I decided the only way we could be truly anonymous was in the middle of the city. We were spectacularly wrong.'

'Tana?'

'My best friend from school. I was going out with her brother and she was going out with his best mate. Teenage hormones, a bottle of vodka, an on-the-ball paparazzi and the rest is history. I don't even like vodka.'

'So as the camera flashes followed you down the street you thought, I know, I'd like to be on the other side?'

'At least I'm in control when I'm the one taking the photos.' The words hung in the air and she sucked in a breath. That hadn't been what she had intended to say—no matter that it was true.

She shifted her weight and carried on hurriedly. 'After school kicked me out I had no qualifications so I went to the local college where, as long as I took English and maths, I could amuse myself. So I did. I took all the art and craft classes I could. But it was photography I loved the most. I stayed on to do the art foundation course and then applied to St Martin's. When they accepted me it felt as if I had found my place at last.'

That moment when she looked through the viewfinder and focused and the whole world fell away. The clarity when the perfect shot happened after hours of waiting. The happiness she evoked with her pictures, when she took a special moment and documented it for eternity.

A chill ran through her and it wasn't just from

the stone. She felt exposed, as if she had allowed him to see, to hear parts of her even her family were locked out of. She pushed off the column, covering her discomfort with brisk movements. 'What about you?' She turned the tables on her interrogator. 'When did you decide you wanted to stand in a lecture theatre and wear tweed?'

'I only wear tweed on special occasions.' That quirk of the mouth of his. It shocked her every time how one small muscle movement could speed her heart up, cause her pulse to start pounding. 'And my cap and gown, of course.'

'Of course.' Daisy tried not to dwell on the disparity in their education. Sure she had a degree, a degree she had worked very hard for, was very proud of. But it was in photography. Her academic qualifications were a little more lacking. She barely had any GCSEs although she had managed to scrape a pass in maths, something a little more respectable in English.

The man next to her had MAs and PhDs and honorary degrees. He had written books that both sold well and were acclaimed for their scholarship. He had students hanging on his every word, colleagues who respected him.

Daisy? She took photos. How could they ever be

equal? How could she attend professional events at his side? Make conversation with academics? She would be an embarrassment.

'I don't think anyone grows up wanting to be a lecturer. I thought we already established that I wanted to be an outlaw when I was a child, preferably a highwayman.'

'Of course.' She kicked herself mentally at the repetition. Say something intelligent, at least something different.

'But growing up somewhere like Hawksley, surrounded by history with literally every step, it was hard not to be enthused. I wanted to take those stories I heard growing up and make them resonate for other people the way they resonated with me. That's what inspires me. The story behind every stone, every picture, every artefact. My period is late medieval. That's where my research lies and what I teach but my books are far more wide ranging.'

'Like the one about Charles II's illegitimate children?' She had actually read his book a couple of years ago on Rose's recommendation. In fact, she'd also read his book on Richard III and his exposé of the myths surrounding Anne Boleyn, the book that had catapulted him into the bestseller lists. But she couldn't think how to tell him without exposing herself. What if he asked for her opinion and her answers exposed just how ignorant she really was?

Or what if he didn't think her capable of forming any opinion at all...?

'Exactly! Those children are actually utterly pivotal to our history. We all know about Henry VIII's desperate search for an heir and how that impacted on the country but Charles' story is much less well known beyond the plague and the fire and Nell Gwyn.' He was pacing now, lit up with enthusiasm. Several tourists stopped to watch, their faces captivated as they listened to him speak.

Daisy snapped him again. Gone was the slightly severe Seb, the stressed, tired Seb. This was a man in total control, a man utterly at home with himself.

'He actually fathered at least seventeen illegitimate children but not one single legitimate child. If he had the whole course of British History might have changed, no Hanoverians, no William of Orange. And of course the influence and wealth still wielded by the descendants of many of those children still permeate British society to this day.'

'Says the earl.'

It was a full-on smile this time, and her stomach tumbled. How had she forgotten the dimple at the corner of his mouth? 'I am fully aware of the irony.'

'Is it personal, your interest? Any chance your own line is descended through the compliant countess?'

'Officially, no. Unofficially, well, there is some familial dispute as to whether we can trace our descendants back to the Norman invasion or whether we are Stuarts. Obviously I always thought the latter, far more of an exciting story for an impressionable boy, the long-lost heir to the throne.

He began walking along the quad and she followed him, brain whirling. 'A potential Stuart! You could be DNA tested? Although that might throw up some odd results. I wonder how many blue-blooded households actually trace their heritage back to a red-blooded stable boy?'

The glimmer in his eye matched hers. 'Now that would make an interesting piece of research. Not sure I'd get many willing participants though.

Maybe the book after this, if I ever get this one finished.'

A book about Hawksley. Such a vivid setting. 'It would make a great TV show.'

'What? Live DNA testing of all the hereditary peers? You have an evil streak.'

'No.' She paused as he turned into a small passageway and began to climb a narrow winding staircase. Daisy looked about her in fascination, at the lead-paned windows and the heavy wooden doors leading off at each landing.

They reached the third landing and he stopped at a door, pulling a key out of his pocket. The discreet sign simply said Beresford. This was his world, even more foreign to her than a castle and a grand estate. Academia, ancient traditions, learning and study and words.

Daisy's breath hitched as he gestured for her to precede him into the room, a rectangular space with huge windows, every available piece of wall space taken up with bookshelves. A comfy and well-loved-looking leather chesterfield sofa was pulled up opposite the hearth and a dining table and six chairs occupied the centre of the room. His surprisingly tidy desk looked out over the quad.

She felt inadequate just standing in here. Out

of place. Numb, she tried to grasp for something to say, something other than: 'Have you read all those books?' Or 'Doesn't your desk look tidy?'

She returned gratefully to their interrupted conversation. 'I was talking about Hawksley, of course. It's the answer to all your problems. Just think of the visitor numbers, although you'd have to rethink the ridiculous weekends only between Whitsun and August Bank Holiday opening times.'

'What's the answer?' His face had shuttered as if he knew what she was going to say and was already barricading himself off from it.

'Your book about Hawksley, how you can see England's history in it.'

He walked over to his desk and picked up the pile of letters and small parcels and began leafing through. 'The book I haven't actually written yet.' His tone was dismissive but she rushed on regardless.

'You should do it as a TV series. You would be an amazing presenter. Why aren't you? You're clever, photogenic, interesting. I'm amazed they haven't snapped you up.'

'Good God, Daisy.' There was no mistaking the look in his eyes now. Disgust, horror, revulsion.

'Despite everything you've been through that's your solution...' He paused and then resumed, his voice cutting. 'I suppose once a celebrity offspring, always a celebrity offspring. You don't think they've offered? That I haven't had a chance to sign myself and my life over? Do you know what it would mean, if I went on TV?'

She shook her head, too hurt by his response to speak.

'I'd be open game. For every paparazzi or blogger or tabloid journalist. They could rake over my life with absolute impunity—and now your life too! Why would I want that? Why would you want that?'

Daisy could feel tears battling to escape and blinked them back. No emotion, that was the deal. And that included hurt. She wouldn't give him the satisfaction of seeing how much his contempt stung. But nor would she let him dismiss her. 'You need to make Hawksley pay and you said yourself land subsidies and a wedding every weekend won't do it. Besides, you write books—popular history books, not dull academic tomes. You don't mind the publicity for those.'

He paused and ran his hands through his hair. 'That's different.'

'Why?'

The question hung there.

She pressed on. 'Your books win prizes, have posters advertising them in bookshops, I've even seen adverts on bus shelters and billboards! You read in public, sign in public, give public lectures. How is that different from a TV series?'

At first she had sounded diffident, unsure of her argument but as she spoke Seb could hear the conviction in her voice. And he had to admit she was making sense. Unwelcome sense but still.

He fixed his eyes on her face, trying to read her. Every day he found out more about her; every day she surprised him. He had thought she was utterly transparent; sweet, a little flaky maybe, desirable sure but not a challenge. But there were hidden depths to Daisy Huntingdon-Cross. Depths he was only just beginning to discover.

'My books are educational.' He cringed inwardly at the pompous words.

She wasn't giving in. 'So is television, done right. More so, you would reach a far bigger audience, teach far more people, inspire more people. I'm not suggesting you pimp yourself on social media—though some historians do and they do it brilliantly. I'm not suggesting reality TV or magazine photoshoots. I'm talking about you, doing what you do anyway.'

Reach more people. Wasn't that his goal? He sighed. 'I didn't plan this.' Seb put down the pile of still-unopened post and wandered over to the window, staring out. 'I didn't think I'd write anything but articles for obscure journals and the kind of books only my peers would read. That's how I started. That's how academic reputations are made.'

'So what changed?'

'I got offered a book deal. It was luck really, an ex-student of mine went into publishing and the editor she was working for wanted a new popular history series. Stacey thought of me and set up a meeting.'

'She wouldn't have thought of you if you hadn't been an inspiring teacher. Not so much luck, more serendipity.' Daisy walked across the room and stood next to him. Without conscious intention he put his hand out and took hers, drawing her in close. Her hand was warm and yielding.

'Maybe.'

'It's just a suggestion, Seb. I know how you feel about courting publicity, I really do. But Dad always says that if you keep your head down and your life clean they'll lose interest. And he's right—just look at my parents. They were wild in their youth, real headline creators just like yours were. The difference is they settled down. They don't sleep around or take drugs or act like divas. They work hard and live quietly—in a crazy, luxurious bubble admittedly! But that's what we've agreed, isn't it? Quiet, discreet lives. If we live like that then there really is nothing to fear.'

Seb inhaled slowly, taking in her calm, reasonable words. Slowly he moved behind her, slipping an arm around her waist to rest on her still-flat stomach. 'They came after you though.' His voice was hoarse.

'We'll just teach the baby not to go out and get drunk in the middle of London when he or she is sixteen. And if it gets my beauty and your brains we should be okay as far as schooling goes.'

'The other way round works just as well. Stop putting yourself down, Daisy. Academic qualifications are meaningless. I think you might be one of the smartest people I know.'

Her hand came down to cover his, a slight

tremor in the fingers grasping his. 'That's the nicest thing anyone has ever said to me.'

'I mean it.' The air around them had thickened, the usual smells he associated with his office, paper, leather and old stone, replaced by her light floral scent: sweet with richer undertones just like its wearer. Desire flooded him and he moved his other hand to her waist, caressing the subtle curve as he followed the line down to her hip.

Seb had no idea how this marriage was going to work in many ways but this he had no qualms about. They had been brought together by attraction and so far it continued to burn hot and deep. He leant forward, inhaling her as he ran a tongue over her soft earlobe, biting down gently as she moaned.

The hand covering his tightened and he could feel her breathing speed up. Reluctantly he left her hip, bringing his hand up to push the heavy fall of hair away from her neck so the creamy nape was exposed. She trembled as he moved in close to press a light kiss on her neck, then another, working his way around to the slim shoulder as his hand slid round to her ribs, splaying out until he felt the full underside of her breast underneath his thumb.

Her breaths were coming quicker as she leant against him, arching into his touch, into his kiss, holding on as she turned round to find his mouth with hers. Warm, inviting, intoxicating. 'Are we allowed to do this here?' she murmured against his mouth as he found the zip at the back of her dress and eased it down the line of her back. Her own hands were tugging at his shirt, moving up his back in a teasing, light caress.

'No one will come in,' he promised, slipping the dress from her shoulders, holding in a groan as one hand continued to tease his back, the other sliding round to his chest. 'We have over an hour before the lecture. Of course, I had promised you lunch…'

'Lunch is overrated.' She pressed a kiss to his throat, her tongue darting out to mark the most sensitive spot as her fingers worked on his shirt buttons.

'In that case, my lady—' he held onto her as she undid the final button, pushing his shirt off him with a triumphant smile '—desk, sofa or table?'

Daisy looked up at him, her eyes luminous with desire. 'Over an hour? Let's try for all three.'

Seb swung her warm, pliant body up. 'I was hoping you'd say that. Let's start over here. I think I need to do some very intensive research...'

CHAPTER EIGHT

'YOU WOULDN'T THINK you were publicity-shy, looking at those. My mother would kill to have that kind of exposure—and she doesn't get in front of a camera for less than twenty thousand a day.'

There were five large posters arrayed along the front of the lecture hall, each featuring the same black and white headshot of Seb. Daisy came to a halt and studied them, her head tilted critically. 'Not bad. Did they ask you to convey serious academic with a hint of smoking hot?'

'That was exactly the brief. Why, do you think I look like a serious academic?'

'I think you look smoking hot and—' she eyed the gaggle of giggling girls posing for selfies alongside the furthest poster '—so do they.'

Seb glanced towards the group and quickly turned away so his back was towards them. 'Just because they are a little dressed up doesn't mean they're not interested in the subject matter. They could be going out afterwards.'

'Sure they could.' Daisy patted his arm. 'And when I went to the very dull lectures on Greek vase painting it was because I thought knowing about classical figures on urns would be very helpful to my future career and not because I had a serious crush on the lecturer.'

She sighed. 'Six weeks of just sitting and staring into those dark brown eyes and visualising our future children. Time very well spent. Of course he was happily married and never even looked twice at me.'

'This is Oxford, Daisy. People come here to learn.'

There was a reproving tone in his voice that hit her harder than she liked, a reminder that this was his world, not hers. 'I didn't say I didn't learn anything. You want to know anything about classical art, I'm your girl.'

'Seb!' Daisy breathed a sigh of relief as a smartly dressed woman came out of the stage door and headed straight for them, breaking up the suddenly fraught conversation. The woman greeted Seb with a kiss on both cheeks. 'I've been looking for you. You're late. How are you?'

Seb returned the embrace then put an arm around Daisy, propelling her forward. 'This is my fiancée, Daisy Huntingdon-Cross. I assume you've got the wedding invite? Daisy, this is Clarissa Winteringham, my agent.'

'So this is your mystery fiancée?' Daisy was aware that she was being well and truly sized up by a pair of shrewd brown eyes. 'Invite received and accepted with thanks. It's nice to meet you, Daisy.'

'Likewise.' Daisy held out her hand and it was folded into a tight grip, the other woman still looking at her intently.

'And what do you do, Daisy?'

Most people would probably have started with *congratulations*. Daisy smiled tightly. 'I'm a photographer.'

'Have you ever thought of writing a book?' The grip was still tight on her hand as Daisy shook her head. 'A photographer who gets propelled into the limelight as a model? Could work well for a young adult audience?'

'I don't think so.' Daisy managed to retrieve her hand. 'Thank you though.'

'I'm sure we could find someone else to write it. You would just need to collaborate on plot and lend your name to it. With *your* parents I'm sure I could get you a good deal.'

Of course Clarissa knew exactly who Daisy was, she wouldn't be much of an agent if she didn't, but it still felt uncomfortable, being so quickly and brutally summed up for her commercial value. 'Seb's the writer in the family and I don't think books about models are really his thing.'

'Shame, cheekbones like yours are wasted behind a camera. We could have done a nice tie-in, maybe a reality TV show. Get in touch if you change your mind. Now, Seb, they're waiting for you inside. Have *you* changed your mind about the BBC offer? You really should call me back when I leave messages.'

So she hadn't been the first person to mention TV? Seb didn't react with the same vehemence he'd shown Daisy earlier when she had made a similar suggestion, just shook his head, smiling, as Clarissa bore him off leaving Daisy to trail behind.

The lecture hall was crammed to capacity, an incongruous mixture of eager-looking students, serious intellectual types and several more groups of girls waving cameras and copies of Seb's latest books; pop culture meeting academia.

Daisy managed to find a seat at the end of a row next to an elderly man who commented loudly to his companion throughout the lecture but, despite the disruptions, the odd camera flashes and the over-enthusiastic laughter from Seb's youthful admirers every time he made any kind of joke, Daisy found that she enjoyed the lecture. Seb's enthusiasm for his subject and engaging manner were infectious.

It was funny how the sometimes diffident man, the private man, came alive in front of an audience, how he held them in the palm of his hand as he took them on a dizzying thousand-year tour of English history using his own family home as a guide. The hour-long talk was over far too quickly.

'He knows his stuff.' The old man turned to Daisy as the hall began to empty. Daisy had been planning to go straight to Seb, but he was surrounded immediately by a congratulatory crowd, including the girls she had seen earlier, all pressing in close, books in hand waiting to be signed.

Seb didn't look as if he minded at all. Hated publicity indeed!

'Yes, he was fascinating, wasn't he?' She'd seen her father perform in front of thousands, seen her mother's face blown up on a giant billboard but had never felt so full of awe. 'He's a great speaker.'

'Interesting theory as well. Do you subscribe to his school of thought on ornamental moats?'

Did she what? About what?

'I…'

'Of course the traditional Marxist interpretation would agree with him, but I wonder if that's too simplistic.'

'Yes, a little.' Daisy's hands were damp; she could feel her hair stick to the back of her neck with fear. *Please don't ask me to do anything but agree with you*, she prayed silently.

'Nevertheless he's a clever man, Beresford. I wonder what he'll do after this sabbatical.'

'Do? Isn't he planning to return here?' Seb hadn't discussed his future plans with her at all; he was far too focused on the castle.

'He says so but I think Harvard might snap him up. It would be a shame to lose him but these young academics can be so impatient, always moving on.'

Daisy sat immobile as the elderly man moved past her, her brain whirling with his words. *Harvard?* Okay, they hadn't discussed much in terms of the future, but surely if Seb was considering moving overseas he'd have mentioned it? She got to her feet, dimly aware that the large hall was emptying rapidly and that Seb was nowhere to be seen.

'There you are, Daisy.' Clarissa glided towards her accompanied by a tall man in his late fifties. 'This is Giles Buchanan, Seb's publisher. Giles, Daisy is Seb's mysterious fiancée. She's a photographer.'

'Creative type, eh? Landscapes or fashion?'

Daisy blinked. 'Er…neither, I photograph weddings.'

'Weddings?' Obviously not the kind of job he expected from Seb's fiancée judging by the look of surprise on his face. Daisy filled in the blanks: too commercial, not intellectual enough.

She'd wanted a chance to look inside Seb's world but now she was here she felt like Alice: too big or too small but either way not right. She stepped out onto the stairs. 'Excuse me, I need some air.'

How on earth was she going to fit in? Say the right things, do the right things, be the right kind of wife? She'd thought being a countess was crazy enough—being the wife of an academic looked like being infinitely worse.

Right now it didn't feel as if there was any

chance at all. The gap between them was too wide and she had no idea if she even wanted to bridge it—let alone work out *how* to do it.

'Table decorations, seating plans, favours, flowers, outfits. We've done it all, Vi. There can't be anything left to plan.' Daisy tucked the phone between her ear and her chin as she continued to browse on her laptop. The wedding was feeling less and less real as it got nearer. It was one day, that was all.

And it felt increasingly irrelevant. The real issue was how the marriage was going to work, not whether Great-aunt Beryl was speaking to Great-uncle Stanley or what to feed the vegetarians during the hog roast.

Seb was right. The marriage was the thing. Not that she was going to tell him that, of course.

Less than a week to go. This was it. Was she prepared to spend the foreseeable part of her future with a man who was still in so many ways a complete stranger?

It wasn't that the nights weren't wonderful. Incredible actually. But was sex enough to base a marriage on?

But it wasn't just sex, was it? There was the

baby too. The sex was a bonus and she needed to remember that. *Stop being greedy, stop wanting more.*

Seb definitely found her desirable. Had promised to respect her. That was a hell of a lot more than many women had at the start of their marriages. So she wasn't sure where she fitted in his professional life or at Hawksley? They didn't have to live in each other's pockets after all.

She was completely and utterly lucky—and that was before you factored in the fact she would be living in a castle and, improbable as it seemed, would be a countess. She just had to start feeling it and stop clinging onto the shattered remnants of her romantic dreams. Start carving out a place for herself at Hawksley, turn it into a home. Into her home.

If only she could help Seb work out how to make it pay. Other estates managed it, even without an eminent historian occupying the master bedroom…

Her sister's exasperated voice broke in on her thoughts. 'Daisy, Rose isn't getting here until the day of the wedding itself so as the only bridesmaid on the same continent it's down to me. I've hinted, Mum's hinted and you have been no help so I am asking you outright. Hen night. What are you wanting?'

Daisy straightened, the phone nearly falling out of her hand as she registered her sister's words. 'I forgot all about the hen night.'

'Sure you did.' Vi sounded sceptical. 'I've seen your scrapbooks, Daise, remember? And lived through twenty-four years of your birthday treats. You've left it too late for the Barcelona weekend or the spa in Ischia. So spa day near here? Night out clubbing in London? We could manage a night in Paris if we book today. You're cutting it awfully fine though. We should have gone yesterday.'

Daisy managed to interrupt her sister. 'Nothing, honestly, Vi. I'm not expecting anything.'

'Nothing?'

'Nope.'

'This isn't a test?' Vi sounded suspicious. 'Like the time you said you didn't want a birthday treat but we were supposed to know that you wanted us to surprise you with tickets to see Busted?'

'I was twelve!' Violet had to wheel that one out.

'Seriously, Daisy. Mum will be so disappointed. She's planned matching tracksuits with our names spelled out in diamanté.'

'Mother wouldn't be seen dead in matching tracksuits!'

'But she will be disappointed. You'll be telling me you're not going on some exotic honeymoon next!'

Daisy stopped dead. Honeymoon? She hadn't even thought about what would happen after the wedding and Seb hadn't mentioned it.

The Maldives, Venice, a small secluded island in the Caribbean, a chateau in the south of France; the destinations of the brides and grooms she had photographed over the last couple of years floated through her mind.

They all sounded perfect—for a couple in love.

It was probably a good thing they had forgotten all about it. A week or two holed up together would be excruciating. Wouldn't it? 'It's all been so quick, we haven't actually thought about a honeymoon yet.'

There was an incredulous pause. 'No hen night, no honeymoon. Daisy, what's going on?'

Daisy thought rapidly. She couldn't have a hen night. She couldn't be around her friends and family pretending to be crazy in love, she couldn't drink and her abstinence might have escaped their sharp eyes so far but nobody was going to believe that she wasn't going to indulge in at least one glass of champagne on her own hen night.

Her eyes fell on the copy of Seb's birth certificate lying on her desk; she'd put it in her bag after their visit to the register office and forgotten to return it to him. Name: Sebastian Adolphus Charles Beresford. How on earth had the Adolphus slipped past her attention? She hoped it wasn't a family name he'd want for their son.

Her eyes flickered on. Date of birth. April twentieth. Hang on…

Why hadn't he mentioned it? Right now she wasn't going to think about that. Not when salvation was lying right in front of her.

'The problem is, Vi, tomorrow's Seb's birthday and I've planned a surprise. And then it's just a few days before the wedding and I don't want a big night out before then. Besides,' she added with an element of truth, 'it wouldn't feel right without Rose. We can do something afterwards.'

'Wednesday night.' Vi wasn't giving up. 'That gives you two days before the wedding and we can do something small. Just you, me and Mum and Skype Rose in. Films and face masks and manicures at your studio?'

That sounded blissful. Dangerous but blissful.

'Okay. But low-key—and I won't be drinking. I'm on a pre wedding detox. For my skin.' That sounded plausible.

'Done. I'll source the girliest films and organise nibbles. Wholesome, vitamin filled, organic nibbles.'

'Thanks, Vi.' She meant it. An evening in with her mother and sister would be lovely. As long as she kept her guard up.

Meanwhile there was the small matter of Seb's birthday and the surprise she was supposed to be organising. Once she had decided just what the surprise actually was.

Something was up.

Daisy was going around with a suppressed air of excitement as if she were holding a huge balloon inside that was going to burst any second.

It should have been annoying. Actually it was a little bit endearing.

Seb stretched out in his old leather wingchair, the vibrant red of the curtains catching his eye. Sherry had not received the Keep Out of My Library vibe and his sanctuary was looking as polished and fresh as the rest of the house. It was actually quite nice not to sneeze every time he pulled out a book although he had preferred the curtains unlaundered. They had been less glaringly bright then.

It wasn't just Sherry. Daisy was quietly but firmly making changes as well: painting the kitchen, opening up the morning room and turning it into a cosy sitting room despite using little more than new curtains and cushions and replacing the rather macabre paintings of dead pheasants with some watercolour landscapes she had rescued from the attics. Although they still lived mainly in the kitchen or library, they had begun to spend their evenings in there reading, watching television or playing a long-running but vicious game of Monopoly.

It was almost homely.

But even as the castle began to take shape he was all too aware there still weren't enough hours in the day. It would be much easier if he brought in a professional to manage the estate, leaving Seb to his teaching and research.

It wasn't the Beresford way though. His grandfather had been very clear on that. A good owner managed his land, his people, his family and his home no matter what the sacrifice. And there had been many throughout the long centuries. There were times when Seb wondered if he would ever be able to return to Oxford and his real work.

Yet at the same time the pull of his ancestral home was so strong. He couldn't carry on juggling both the estate and academia but making a final decision was unthinkable.

He looked up at the sound of a soft tap on the door, relieved to take his eyes off the blank laptop screen. He had barely achieved anything yet again, he noted wryly. Worries and thoughts circling round and round; even his research wasn't distracting him the way it usually did. Money, Daisy, the baby, Hawksley, the book. In less than six months his whole life had turned upside down.

Although if he hadn't allowed himself to be so distracted by his career maybe Hawksley at least wouldn't be in such a state. He had his own culpability here.

The door opened and Daisy appeared bearing one of the massive silver tea trays. One mobile brow flew up as she looked at him. 'That's a terrifying scowl. Am I interrupting a crucial moment?'

'You're interrupting nothing but mental flailing and flagellation.' He tried to smile. 'Sorry if I scared you.'

'Mental flagellation? Sounds painful. Anything I can help with?' She carried the tray over to the table in the opposite corner and set it down with an audible thud.

'Not unless you have a time machine.'

Seb regretted the words as soon as he uttered them; he didn't need the flash of hurt to cross her face to show him how ill-judged they were. 'Not you, not the baby.' Not entirely. 'Goodness knows, Daisy, out of all the crazy tangled mess my life has become the baby is the one bright spot. No, I was just thinking if I'd acted sooner then things would be a hell of a lot easier now.'

'How so?'

He pushed his laptop away and sat back in the chair trying to straighten out his skein of thoughts and regrets. 'Kids are selfish, aren't they? I spent my holidays here, school and university—unless my mother was suffering one of her occasional fits of maternal solicitude, but I was so wrapped up in the past I never took an interest in the present. Never saw how Grandfather was struggling, never tried to help.' He suppressed a deep sigh of regret.

'History is all well and good but it's not very practical, is it? Grandfather suggested I go to the local agricultural college and do estate management, come and work here. I brushed him off, convinced I was destined for higher things.'

'You were right.' She was perched on the arm of the old leather chair, legs crossed, and his eyes ran appreciably up the long bare limbs. She was wearing the black tweed shorts, this time teamed with a bright floral shirt and her trademark hat was a cap pulled low over her forehead.

'Was I?' He had been sure then, sure throughout his glittering career. But the past few months had shown just how flawed his ambition had been. 'Hawksley needed new blood, Grandfather was struggling and my father was never going to step in. My grandfather was too proud to ask me directly and I was too busy to notice. But maybe I could have helped him turn things around—and been on the ground to stop my father's gross negligence.'

It was more than negligence. His father's wilful use of estate capital had been criminal.

'How could you have stopped it?'

'The money funding his extravagant lifestyle came from a family trust. It was never intended for private use, certainly not on his scale. Just one look at the accounts would have alerted me.' And he could have stepped in.

'I was far too busy chasing my own kind of fame.' The taste in his mouth was bitter.

She swung her legs down and hopped to her feet. 'Just because he suggested estate management doesn't mean he was desperate for you to live and work here. He was proud of you no matter which path you chose.'

'I wish I believed that.' His mouth twisted. 'I guess we'll never know.'

'I know.' She went over to one of the shelves, pulling a hardback book out. 'This is yours, isn't it? The first one? Look how well read it is, the spine is almost broken. So unless you spend your evenings reading your own words I think your grandparents must have read it. Several times.'

He took the book from her outstretched hands. He had given it to them, signed it and handed it over unsure if they would ever read it. The hardback was battered, corners turned, the pages well thumbed. A swell of pride rose inside him. Maybe they had been proud of his chosen career. He looked over at Daisy. 'Thank you.'

'I knew this library was all for show. If you ever looked at a book you'd have seen it for yourself,' but her eyes were bright and the corners of her full mouth upturned.

'Anyway—' she walked back to the tray '—I have a small bone to pick with you, my Lord. Why didn't you tell me it was your birthday?'

Seb gaped at her in shock. 'How did you know?'

'Incredible detective skills and a handy copy of your birth certificate. In my family birthdays are a very big deal.' She turned with a shy smile, her hands behind her back. 'And I must warn you I have very high expectations for mine, just ask my sisters, so if we are going to be a family—' the colour rose high on her cheeks and her eyes lowered as she said the words '—then your birthday has to be a big deal as well. So. Happy Birthday.'

With a flourish she pulled her arms from behind her back. One held a plate complete with a large cupcake, a lit candle on the top, the other a shiny silver envelope.

He stood, paralysed with surprise. 'What's this?'

'It's a card and cake. These are usual on birthdays.' Her colour was still high but her voice was light. 'You're supposed to blow the candle out.'

He just stood there, unable to move a muscle, to process what she was saying. 'I haven't had a birthday cake since I was ten. I was always at school, you see.'

Her eyes softened. 'The procedure hasn't changed. You blow, the flame goes out, I clap and then we eat it. Simple.'

He made a huge effort to reach out and took the plate of cake, holding it gingerly as if it were a bomb about to explode. The small flame danced before his eyes. He didn't want to blow it out; he wanted to watch it twist and turn for ever. 'And the card?'

'That you open. And then we get changed. I have a surprise for you. And I am quite convinced it is going to blow your socks off.'

CHAPTER NINE

'How did you know that this is my favourite band?' Seb, Daisy was learning, was not a huge one for words. If someone arranged a surprise for Daisy she found it hard to sit back and wait; instead she would be peppering them with questions, trying to guess where they were going, slightly anxious it wasn't going to live up to her own fevered imaginings.

Seb had just looked bemused, as if the concept of a surprise trip was completely alien to him. Which was ridiculous. He might not want high emotions or romance but he'd had girlfriends before—had none of them ever organised a day out? To a special library or a site of special historical significance?

But even his slightly annoying calm and collected manner had disappeared when the taxi pulled into the concert venue.

'Seriously, Daisy. You must be some kind of witch.' His hand sought hers and squeezed, his touch tingling. For a brief moment she allowed herself to fantasise that this was real, that she was on a night out with someone she was mad about, with someone who was mad about her.

'Yes, I am. My spells include listening to the music that people play and reading the labels on CD collections.' She couldn't help it, music had been such a huge part of her childhood she sub-consciously noticed whatever music was playing although she didn't play an instrument herself and rarely listened to music for pleasure, preferring silence as she worked.

But Seb liked background noise whether in the kitchen, his study or driving around and when she had been searching the internet, trying to find something to do tonight, the name had jumped out at her—it had been the CD he was playing that very first night. One call to her father later and VIP seats had been procured.

But it had evidently been the perfect gift. Daisy was torn between shame that all she had managed was a last-minute, hastily organised event and a sneaking fear that maybe she knew him better than she had realised, than she wanted to admit.

Knew exactly what would make him happy. That would involve caring. Was that part of their deal?

Seb was evidently not having any deep thoughts or misgivings. It was fun to see him enjoying every moment like a child set free in a toy shop as they were led through the plush VIP area. 'A box? Seriously?'

'You may have the title but I am rock aristocracy and this is how we experience concerts,' she told him as they took their seats. 'If you would prefer to stand on the beer-covered floor with all the other sweaty people then you can. Your wristband allows you access.'

She could tell he was tempted. Daisy had never understood the allure of the mosh pit herself.

'Maybe later. You wouldn't mind?'

She shook her head. 'Knock yourself out.'

He looked around in fascination and Daisy tried to see it through his eyes, not her own jaded viewpoint. They were the only occupants of a box directly opposite the stage. Behind them was a private room complete with bar and cloakroom. The entire row was taken up with similar boxes for celebrities and friends and family of the band; corporates were restricted to the row above. Access to their coveted seats was strictly controlled.

'This is crazy.' Seb was staring at the aging rock star and his much-younger girlfriend enthusiastically making out in the next-door box. Daisy sat back; she hoped the rock star hadn't seen her. She'd been flower girl at his third wedding—and his new girlfriend looked younger than Daisy herself. 'I've been to plenty of events, literary events, historical conferences, Oxford balls but never anything like this.

'But I would have been just as happy on the beer-soaked floor with the other sweaty people,' he said. He meant it too.

'I'm spoiled,' she admitted. 'Dad gets tickets to everything and always took us along. I'd been to more concerts than films by the time I was ten. He drew the line at boy bands though. That's probably why they remain my own guilty pleasure. But I haven't done anything like this for ages.'

'Why not? If I had free access to gigs I'd go to everything!'

He wouldn't. Not with the high price tag. 'I don't usually like to ask for favours. Mum can get me anything, the new must-have bag or coat or dress—but the deal is you get photographed wearing it. If, like me, you want a quiet life then the price for a freebie is far too high. But tickets for this sold out months ago so it was best seats in the house or nothing!'

Daisy crossed her fingers, hoping that they weren't papped while they were here. There were far more gossip-worthy couples out in force; hopefully the spotlight would be far from them.

'Well, if we must sit in luxury while free drinks and food are pressed on us then I suppose we must. Seriously, Daisy. Thank you. This is incredibly thoughtful.'

Daisy shifted uncomfortably, guilt clamping her stomach. Not so much thoughtful as expedient. She hurriedly changed the subject. 'I'm going to spend Wednesday night at the studio. Vi was insistent that I have some kind of hen night. Obviously I didn't want anything big so it's going to be a family-only films and pampering night. I've told her I'm not drinking for the sake of my skin. I must be more of a demanding bride than I realised. She completely bought it. I might stay there Thursday night too. It's meant to be bad luck to spend the night before together.'

'I guess we need all the luck we can get.' His voice was dry.

'Are you going to have a stag night?'

The shock on his face was almost comical. 'It hadn't even occurred to me! Maybe I should go to the local pub for a couple of drinks—just to add convincing detail to the wedding.'

'What a method actor you are.' But the rest of her conversation with Violet was running through her mind. 'Vi also asked about the honeymoon.'

Seb froze; she could see his knuckles turn white and hurried on. 'I said that we were planning something later on and were too busy right now. I don't think she's wholly convinced but when I tell them about the baby I'm sure they'll forget all about whether we did or did not go away.'

'Do you want a honeymoon?'

To her horror Daisy felt her mouth quiver. She gulped down an unexpected sob as it tried to force its way out. She had told herself so many times that she was at peace with her decision, that she was almost happy with her situation—and then she'd be derailed and have to start convincing herself all over again. 'Of course not.' She could hear the shakiness of her voice. 'I think we're doing brilliantly under the circumstances but a honeymoon might be a bit too much pressure.'

'Are you sure?'

She nodded, hoping he wasn't looking too closely. That he didn't see the suspicious shine in her eyes as she blinked back tears. 'Besides, I'm pregnant. No cocktails on the beach or exotic climates for me.'

'Is that what you would want?'

Yes. Of course it was. That was what people did, wasn't it? Flew to beautiful islands and drank rum and snorkelled in the sun, making love all night in a tangle of white sheets on mahogany beds.

Lovely in theory. Would the reality live up? 'Actually, I think I would want something a little less clichéd. Amazing scenery I could photograph, good food. History. The Alps maybe, Greece, the Italian coast.'

'A friend of mine has a villa on Lake Garda, right on the water's edge. I could see if it's free?'

For one moment she wavered. The Italian lakes. A private villa overlooking the lake sounded sublime. But they would still be pretending and without their work, without the routine of their everyday lives, how would they manage? 'No.' Her voice was stronger. 'Honestly. I'm absolutely fine.'

To her relief as she said the words the lights went down and Seb leaned forward, all his attention on the stage in front, leaving Daisy free to imagine a different kind of honeymoon. One where both parties wanted to be there, were so wrapped up in each other that they didn't need anyone or anything else. The kind of honeymoon she had always dreamed of and now knew she would never have.

It just wasn't adding up.

The Georgian part of the castle needed a new roof, ideally rewiring and, with the baby due before Christmas, Seb really should sort out some of the ancient plumbing problems as well.

The work he had been doing on the estate land was already paying dividends and the farms and forests were looking healthy. It was just the castle.

Just. Just one thousand years of history, family pride and heritage. No big deal.

Seb tried to avoid his grandfather's eye, staring balefully out of a portrait on the far wall. He knew how much his grandfather had hated the idea of using the castle for profit—but surely he would have hated it falling around his ears much more.

But how far could Seb go? He was allowing a location agency to put the castle on their books, ready to hire it out for films and TV sets. It felt like a momentous step.

But not a big enough one.

Meanwhile there was the book to finish researching—and he was already halfway through his sabbatical. Just returning to Oxford for a day had reminded him how time consuming his teaching and administrative duties were.

Something was going to have to give and soon. It wasn't an easy decision.

'Seb, darling?' Sherry had materialised by his side. How on earth was the woman so dammed soft-footed? It was most unnerving.

Seb gripped the edge of his desk and took a deep breath, trying not to show his irritation. There were still three days to go until the wedding and he hadn't had ten uninterrupted minutes since breakfast. 'I have no idea, ask Daisy.' Whatever the question she was bound to know the answer.

'I haven't seen Daisy all morning.' Sherry frowned. 'Really, Seb. It would be helpful if one of you took an interest. These details may seem unimportant but they matter. A high bow at the top of the chair can be smart but rather showy. A lower one is classier maybe but can be lost. Especially with the pale yellow you've chosen.'

He'd chosen? Things might have changed at an alarming speed but there was one thing Seb knew for sure—he had had nothing whatsoever to do with choosing the colour of ribbons for the backs of chairs.

'Let's go for classy.' He rubbed his eyes. If anyone had suggested a month ago that he would be sitting in his library discussing bows with a supermodel he would have poured them a stiff brandy and suggested a lie-down. Yet here he was—and this particular supermodel wasn't going anywhere until he gave her the answer she wanted.

'You're probably right.' She reached over and ruffled his hair in a maternal way, incongrous coming from the glamorous Sherry Huntingdon. 'Classy is always best. Less is more, as I told the girls when they were growing up.'

'Wise advice.' But something she had said earlier was nagging at him. 'Where's Daisy gone?'

'I have no idea. She said she was tired after last night and wandered off. She did look peaky. There's a lovely picture of you two on the *Chronicle Online*. You do scrub up nicely, Seb. It's good to see you make an effort. There's no need to take the absent-minded-academic thing quite so seriously, you know.' Sherry gave his old worn shirt a pointed look.

'Hmm?' But he had already reached for the phone she was holding out, stomach lurching as he scrolled through the *Chronicle*'s long list of celebrity sightings and pictures. There they were entering the concert venue last night: Daisy long-legged in black shorts and a red T-shirt, her lipstick as bright as her top and her favourite trilby pushed back on her head. Seb had been unsure what to wear and had plumped for black trousers and a charcoal-grey shirt. Daisy's arm was linked through his and she was laughing. To a casual observer—and to the headline writer—they looked very much the happy couple.

He thrust the phone back at Sherry. 'Why are they even interested? So we go to a concert, what's the big deal?'

'You have to admit it's a fairy-tale romance, rock star's daughter marrying an earl after just a few weeks.' Her voice was calm but the sharp gleam in her eyes showed her own curiosity. 'Of course they're interested. It'll die down.'

'Will it?' He could hear the bitter note in his voice and made an effort to speak more normally. 'I hope so.'

With in-laws like the ones he would shortly be acquiring, any chance of anonymity seemed very far away.

Sherry drifted away, her long list wafting from

one elegant hand, and Seb tried to turn his attention back to his laptop. But once again his attention wandered. Where *was* Daisy?

She had slept in her own room last night citing tiredness. His own bed had seemed so huge, empty. Cold. At one point he had rolled over, ready to pull her into his arms—only she hadn't been there. It was odd how her absence had loomed through the long, almost sleepless night.

Odd how quickly he had grown accustomed to her presence; the low, even breathing, the warmth of her. The way she woke up spooned into him, the long hair spread over both pillows.

Odd how right it felt.

She hadn't shown up for breakfast either. Seb drummed his fingers on the desktop, the leather soft under his persistent touch. She had looked so vibrant in the photo but at some point in the evening her usual exuberance had dimmed and she had hardly said a word on the way back to Hawksley.

He cast his mind back, trying to remember the conversation of the night before. What had they talked about?

Had it been the mention of the honeymoon? The honeymoon she didn't want.

The honeymoon she didn't want to take with him.

Maybe she was wrong. Maybe they needed this, time away from the pressures of work and family, time away from putting on their best manners and working hard to fit their lives together—maybe it was time to find out how they operated as a couple. He would discuss it again with her.

Only… His fingers drummed a little harder as he thought. She had surprised him last night and it had been one of the most thoughtful things anyone had ever done for him. Maybe it was time for Seb to return the favour.

He pulled the laptop towards him, not allowing himself time to think things through and change his mind, quickly typing in Gianni's email address. Subject heading 'Lake Garda'.

He might not be her dream fiancé but Daisy deserved the perfect honeymoon and he was going to make sure she had it. It was the least he could do.

He had expected to find her in the kitchen. Daisy had been forbidden from doing any of the actual sanding herself. Seb was pretty sure all the dust wasn't good for the baby, but it didn't stop her superintending every job. Under her instructions the walls had been repainted a creamy white, the sanded and restored cupboards, cabinets and dresser a pale grey. He'd been sceptical about the colour but, walking into the warm, soothing space, he had to admit she was right.

The estate joiner had been hard at work planing and oiling wood from one of the old oaks that had fallen in the winter storms, creating counter tops from the venerable old tree. It seemed fitting that a tree that had stood sentry in the grounds for so many generations should be brought inside and used for the changing of the guard.

Daisy had found an old clothes rack in one of the outbuildings and had arranged for it to be suspended from the ceiling, hanging the old copper saucepans from it. She had unearthed his great-grandmother's tea set from the attic and arranged it on the shelves, the old-fashioned forget-me-not pattern blending timelessly with the creams and greys. The overall effect was of useful comfort. A warm, family kitchen, a place for work and conversation. For sweet smells and savoury concoctions, for taking stock of the day while planning the next.

The kitchen had been changing day by day and yet he hadn't really taken in the scale of her efforts. It wasn't just that the kitchen was freshly restored, nor that it was scrupulously clean. It wasn't just the new details like the pictures on the wall, old landscapes of the grounds and the castle, the newly installed sofa by the Aga and the warm rug Monty had claimed for his own. It was the feeling. Of care, of love.

The same feeling that hit him when he walked into her rooms, cluttered, sweet-smelling and alive. The same feeling she had created in the morning room and in the library where she had removed some of the heavier furniture and covered the backs of his chairs with warm, bright throws, heaped the window seats high with cushions.

His home was metamorphosing under his eyes and yet he'd barely noticed.

He should tell her he liked the changes.

Seb poured himself a glass of water and sat at the table, thinking of all the places she could have disappeared to. He didn't blame her for wanting some breathing space before the wedding; but if even Sherry couldn't run her to earth Daisy must have chosen her hiding space with care.

Neatly piled on the tabletop were some of the old scrapbooks and pictures Sherry had printed out from Daisy's website and internet pin boards. Seb reached out curiously and began to leaf through them. He expected to see a little girl's fantasy, all meringues and Cinderella coaches.

Instead he was confronted by details: a single flower bound in ribbon, a close-up of an intricate piece of lace, an embellished candle. Simple, thoughtful yet with a quirky twist. Like Daisy herself.

A piece of paper fell out and he picked it up. It was a printed-out picture of a ring: twisted pieces of fine gold wire embellished with fiery stones. A million miles away from the classic solitaire he had presented her with.

A solitaire she rarely wore. She was worried she'd lose it, she said. But it wasn't just that; he could see it in her eyes.

He hadn't known her at all when he'd bought it for her. Picked out a generic ring, expensive, sure, flawless—but nothing special, nothing unique. He could have given that ring to anyone.

And Daisy was definitely not just anyone.

Seb leant back, the picture in his hand. He really should show her just how much he appreciated all that she had done.

She was so busy trying to fit in with him, to turn his old house into a home. It was time he gave something back. The wedding of her dreams, the honeymoon of her dreams.

The ring of her dreams.

It wasn't the full package, he was all too aware of that. But it was all he had, wasn't it? It would have to do.

He just hoped it would be enough.

CHAPTER TEN

THERE IT WAS. Daisy sucked in a long breath, forcing herself to stay low and remain still, remain quiet despite every nerve fizzing with excitement. Slowly, carefully, she focused the zoom lens.

Click.

The otter didn't know it was being photographed—much like Daisy herself last night. Would the otter feel as violated, as sick to its stomach if she published the shot on her website?

Had Seb seen it? Each time a photo of them appeared in the press he got a little colder, a little more withdrawn and she could feel herself wither with each snap too.

Was it the intrusion itself she minded—or the image portrayed in the pictures? They looked so happy last night, hands clasped, heads turned towards each other, as if they were wrapped up in their own world, totally complete together.

And they said the camera never lied...

Daisy shook off the thought, allowing her own

camera to follow the sleek mammal as it swam up the river, turning giddy somersaults in the water, playing some game she longed to understand. Was it lonely, swimming all by itself? Maybe by the summer it would have cubs to play with. She hoped so.

Her mind drifted down to the new life inside her. Still so small, only perceptible by the swelling in her breasts and sensitivity to certain smells and yet strong, growing, alive. 'Will I be less lonely when you're here?' she whispered.

It was a terrible burden to put on a baby. Happiness and self-fulfilment. Daisy focused again on the gliding otter. She had her camera, her work, her family. That was enough. It had to be enough.

Only. What if it wasn't? She was trying so hard. Trying to be calm and sensible and fit in with the slow and steady pace of life at Hawksley she glimpsed between wedding preparations: Seb with his research, Seb out in the fields, talking to tenants, the weekend tourists herded around the small areas open to the public. It was as distant from her busy London life as the otter's life was from an urban fox's streetwise existence.

She was making a list of the most immediate refurbishments needed in the house and was happily delving deep into the crammed attics. But despite everything Seb said she didn't feel as if she had a right to start making changes; it felt as if she were playing at being the lady of the house. She was still a visitor, just a momentary imprint in the house's long history.

And although Seb hadn't gone into great detail she knew that money was tight, the trust set up to keep the castle depleted, ransacked in return for a jet-set existence. Seb had to wait for probate before he could start to sell off all the luxury items his parents had lavished their money on. Until they were sold it was impossible to know just how much she could draw on. Right now she was doing her best with things scavenged from the attic, materials she could turn into cushions or curtains, pictures that just needed a polish.

Hawksley needed far more work than easy cosmetic fixes. How could she plan the renovations it needed when she knew full well the cost would be exorbitant?

It was hard to grasp how life would be afterwards. The wedding overshadowed everything, created buzz and fuss and work and life. Once Sherry left for good, the vows were said and the marquee tidied away what would be left for her?

Would she find herself desperate to shout out loud, to stand in the middle of the courtyard and scream, to tear the calm curtain of civility open? To get some reaction somehow.

The wedding was just a day. She had the rest of her life here to navigate.

And there was nobody to discuss it with. Seb didn't want emotions in his life and she had agreed to respect that. This fear of loneliness, emotions stretching to breaking point, was exactly the kind of thing he abhorred.

And of course, where there wasn't emotion there couldn't be love. Could there?

Daisy got slowly to her feet, careful not to disturb the still-basking otter. Love? Where had that come from? She knew full well that love wasn't on offer in this pact of theirs. It was just…

There was passion behind that serious, intellectual face. She had known it that very first night. Had seen it again time after time. Not just in bed but in his work, his attachment to his home. And passion was emotion…

Seb might not think that he did emotion but he did. His books were bestsellers because they brought the past alive. No one could write with such sensual sensitivity about the lusts of the Stuart court without feeling the hunger himself.

There were times when the almost glacial green eyes heated up, darkened with need. Times when the measured voice grew deeper, huskier. Times when sense was tossed aside for immediacy. Seb desired her, she knew that. Desire was an emotion.

Of course he was capable of love! Just not for her. Maybe, if she hadn't interrupted the steady pace of his life, he would have met somebody suitable. Someone who shared his love for the past, who would have known how to overcome his fears, helped to heal his hurts.

He'd been robbed of his chance for love just as she had. They were in this together.

And so she wouldn't dwell on the way her stomach lurched every time he looked directly at her, on the way her skin fizzed at every causal touch. She wouldn't allow herself to think about how he made her feel smart as well as sexy. As if she counted.

Because that way lay madness and regret. That way led to revelations she wasn't ready to face. That way led to emotions and maybe Seb was right. Maybe emotions were too high a price to pay. Maybe stability was what mattered.

'Where have you been?' Daisy started as she heard the slightly irritable voice. She bit back a near hysterical giggle. Think of the devil and he will come.

'I've been looking everywhere. Your mother is worried. Says she hasn't seen you all morning and that you look tired.' His gaze was intent, as if he were searching out every shadow in her face. In her soul.

'I just couldn't face any more in-depth discussions about whether as Violet's best friend Will should count as her date, or if Vi and Rose should have the same hairstyle so I came out for some air.' It wasn't a total lie. The nearer the wedding got, the more she wanted to run. Funny to think that once she had planned for this, thought all these tiny details mattered.

Now she just wanted it over and done with.

'Some air?' Seb bit back a smile. 'You're almost at the edge of the estate. I couldn't believe it when Paul said he'd seen you walk this way.'

'I like it down here. It's peaceful.' The river wound around the bottom of the wooded valley, Hawksley invisible on the other side of the hill. Here she was alone, away from the fears and the worries and the nerves.

'It used to be one of my favourite places when I was younger. There's a swimming spot just around that bend.'

'Shh! Look!' Daisy grabbed his arm and pointed. 'There's another one. Do you think they're mates? Do otters live in pairs?' She dropped his arm to pull her camera back up, focusing and clicking over and over.

'Not European otters.' Seb spoke in a low even tone as they watched the pair duck and dive, their sinewy bodies weaving round each other in an underwater dance. 'They're very territorial so I think we might be lucky enough to see a mating pair—in two months' time there could be cubs. They actually mate underwater.'

'It looks like she's trying to get away.'

'The dog otters often have to chase the females until she agrees.'

'Typical males!'

They stood there for a few minutes more, almost unable to breathe trying not to alert the couple to their presence until, at last, the female otter took off around the bend in the river doggedly pursued by the male and the pair were lost from sight.

'That was incredible.' Daisy turned to Seb. His eyes reflected her own awe and wonderment, the same incredulous excitement. 'I can't believe we were lucky enough to witness that.'

'Do you think he's caught her?'

She tossed her head. 'Only if she wants him to. But I hope she did. What a project that would make—documenting the mating dance right through to the cubs maturing.'

'I didn't know you were into nature photography?'

His words brought back the look of utter incomprehension on his publisher's face. Nature photography, high fashion, art—they were intellectual pursuits, worthy. Weddings, romance? They just didn't cut it.

'I'm into anything wonderful, anything beautiful.' She turned away, a mixture of vulnerability and anger replacing the excitement, then turned back again to face him, to challenge him. 'What, you thought I was too shallow to appreciate nature?'

He gripped her shoulders, turning her to face him, eyes sparkling with anger of his own. 'Don't put words into my mouth, Daisy.'

'But that's what you meant, wasn't it?' She twisted away from his touch, acidic rage, corrosive and damaging, churning her stomach. 'A nature photographer wife would be so much more fitting for you than a wedding photographer. So much more intellectual than silly, frivolous romance.'

'How on earth did you reach that crazy conclusion? This has nothing to do with me.' Seb dropped his hands, stepped back, mouth open in disbelief. 'It's to do with you. Why do you always do this? Assume everyone else thinks the worst of you? The only person who puts you down, Daisy Huntingdon-Cross, is you. Photograph babies or weddings or cats or otters. I don't care. But don't take all your insecurities and fasten them on me. I won't play.'

'Why? Because that would mean getting involved?' Daisy knew she was making no sense, knew she was stirring up emotions and feelings that didn't need to be disturbed. That she was almost creating conflict for the sake of it. But she couldn't stop. 'God forbid that the high and mighty Earl of Holgate actually feel something. Have an opinion on another person.'

Seb took another step back, his mouth set firm, his eyes hard. 'I won't do this, Daisy. Not here, not now, not ever. I told you, this is not how I will live. If you want to fight, go pick a quarrel with your mother but don't try and pick one with me.'

Daisy trembled, the effort of holding the words in almost too much. But through the tumult and silent rage another emotion churned. Shame. Because Seb was right. She was trying to pick a quarrel, trying to see if she could get him to react.

And he was right about something else. She was fastening her own insecurities on him. He was very upfront about her job; he mocked it, laughed at it but he *had* supported her when she'd needed it. And he might think weddings frivolous but he had commented on some of her photos, praised the composition.

'I was being unfair.' The words were so soft she wasn't sure if she had actually said them aloud. 'I don't know if it's the stress of the wedding or pregnancy hormones or lack of sleep. But I'm sorry. For trying to provoke you.'

He froze, a wary look on his face. 'You are?'

Her mouth curved into a half smile. 'I grew up with two sisters, you know. This is how we operated—attack first.'

'Sounds deadly.' But the hard look in his eyes had softened. 'Are you ready to walk back? If you're very lucky I'll show you where I used to build my den.'

Daisy recognised the conciliatory note for what it was and accepted the tacit peace offering. 'That sounds cool. We had treehouses but they were constructed for us, no makeshift dens for us.'

'I can imagine.' His tone was dry. Whatever he was imagining probably wouldn't be too far from the truth. They had each had their own, ornate balconied structures constructed around some of the grand old oaks in Huntingdon Hall's parkland.

They strode along, Seb pointing out objects of interest as Daisy zoomed in on some of the early signs of spring budding through the waking woodland. The conversation was calm, non-consequential, neither of them alluding to the brief altercation.

And yet, Daisy couldn't help thinking, he had been the first to react. Immediate and unmistakeable anger. In his eyes, in his voice, in the grip on her shoulders, in his words. She had got to him whether he admitted it or not. Was that a good thing? A breakthrough?

She had no idea. But it was proof that he felt something. What that actually was remained to be seen but right now she would take whatever she could get.

Because it meant hope.

'These are really good, Daisy.'

'Mmm.' But she sounded critical as she continued to swipe through the files. Seb had no idea why. Whether the pictures were colour or black and white she had completely captured the otters' essence. Watching the photos in their natural order was like being told a story.

She obviously felt about her photos the way he felt about his words—no matter how you tinkered and played and edited they could always be better.

Daisy pulled a face and deleted a close-up that looked perfect to him. 'What I need down there is a proper hide. Preferably one with cushions and a loo.'

It would be the perfect spot. 'I did consider putting in a nature trail, but it means more people coming onto the land.'

'And that's a problem, why?' She looked up from the laptop, her gaze questioning.

He bit back the surge of irritation, trying to keep his voice even. 'This is my home, Daisy. How would you like people traipsing all over Hunting-don Hall at all times of the day?'

She leant back, the blue eyes still fixed on him. 'We often open up the hall. Mum and Dad host charity galas and traditionally the hall is the venue for the village fete plus whatever else the village wants to celebrate—and there's always some-thing. Besides, yes, they do own some parkland and the gardens are huge by nearly anyone else's standards but it doesn't even begin to compare to Hawksley. Don't you think you're a bit selfish keeping it locked up?'

Selfish? Words were Seb's trade—and right now he had lost his tools. All he could do was stare at her, utterly nonplussed. 'I let people look around the castle.'

She wrinkled her nose and quoted: '"Restricted areas of the house are available to members of the public from eleven a.m. until three p.m., weekends only between Whitsun and September the first."'

Okay, the hours were a *little* restrictive. 'I hire out the Great Hall.'

'Saturdays only. And you don't allow anyone else onto the estate apart from the villagers and your tenants.'

His defensive hackles rose as she continued.

It was as if she had looked into all his worries and was gradually exhuming each one. 'That's how we've always done things.' An inadequate response, he knew, but until he made some difficult decisions it was all he had.

'I know.' She looked as if she wanted to continue but instead closed her mouth with a snap, continuing to flick through the photos.

'But?' he prompted.

'But things are different now. You need to start running the estate as a commercial enterprise, not as a gentleman's hobby.'

Ouch. 'What do you think I've been doing these last few months?' he demanded. 'Research? I have barely touched my book. I've been doing my damnedest to try and get all the farming grants I can…'

'That's not going to be enough.' She bit her lip and looked down at her screen, clearly thinking hard about something. 'I didn't want to show you this until I had done more work on it. It's not ready yet.'

'Show me what?' Wariness skittered down his spine.

She clicked on the screen and swivelled the laptop round so he could see the screen.

Seb had expected a photo. Instead a formatted slide complete with bullet points faced him. He raised an eyebrow. 'PowerPoint?'

Daisy coloured. 'I know it's a little OTT but I couldn't think how else to order it.'

'Go on, then. Amaze me.' He knew he sounded dismissive but, honestly, what on earth could a wedding photographer who was expelled from school at sixteen contribute to the ongoing Hawksley struggle that he hadn't considered? But, he conceded, if this was going to be her home he should at least listen to whatever crackpot ideas she had dreamed up.

She chewed on her lip for a moment, looking at him doubtfully before taking a deep breath and pointing one slim finger at the screen.

'Okay.' She slid him a nervy glance. 'I want you to have an open mind, okay?'

He nodded curtly even as he felt his barriers go up.

'This is Chesterfield Manor. The house, grounds and estate are a similar size to Hawksley. Chesterfield Manor has been open to the public for the last fifteen years. They specialise in outdoor trails and natural play.' She sounded self-conscious, as if she were reading from a script.

'An insurance nightmare.'

'This one…' The slide showed a magnificent Tudor house. 'This is known for productions of plays, especially Shakespeare and they also do themed medieval banquets.'

'In costume? Tell me you aren't serious!'

Daisy didn't reply, just carried on showing him slide after slide of stately homes spread throughout the UK ranging from a perfectly preserved Norman Castle to a nineteenth-century gothic folly, her manner relaxing as she settled into the presentation, pointing out all the various ways they attracted paying visitors.

Seb's heart picked up speed as he looked at each slide, hammering so hard it rivalled the tick of the old grandfather clock in the hallway.

Everything she was showing him he had considered. Every conclusion she had drawn he had already drawn—and rejected. Too risky, not in keeping. A betrayal of his grandfather's already squandered legacy.

Risks and spending money without thought of the consequences had almost broken Hawksley once.

Allowing the cameras into their home had just fuelled his parents' narcissism, and greed.

He couldn't go down that road. Didn't she understand that?

He had thought she understood.

He had obviously been very wrong…

Seb took in a deep breath, stilling his escalating pulse, and sat back and folded his arms. 'So people like stately homes.'

'Hawksley has two things none of these have.' She waited expectantly.

He sighed. 'Which are?'

'Its utterly unique appearance—and you. An eminent historian in situ right here. Look, I've been talking to Paul…'

His eyes narrowed. 'You have been busy.'

She lifted her chin. 'The farms pay for themselves, the village pays for itself—but the castle is in deficit. You can apply for as many grants as you like but that's not going to fix the roof and certainly won't replace the money your father squandered. The income from the trust used to pay for all the castle's bills and living expenses for the earl and his family—right now you'd find it hard to replace the toaster.'

It was an exaggeration but his gut tightened at her words. Did she think he didn't know this?

Didn't lie awake night after night thinking of every which way he could solve it?

'But, Seb, there are so many ways we could use the castle to generate the income it needs. Start using the keep, as well as the hall, for weddings and parties too—erect a wooden and canvas inner structure inside the walls just like they did at Bexley. Hold plays, open all week Easter to September and weekends out of season. Have a Christmas open house.' She hesitated. 'Allow tours of the main house.'

Seb's chest tightened at the very thought of strangers wandering around his house. 'No!'

She hurried on. 'I don't mean open access but "pay in advance and reserve your place" tours. Put in a farm shop and nature trails and play parks. We could convert some of the outbuildings into holiday cottages and bridal accommodation.'

'With what?'

'There's some capital left.'

He stared. 'You want me to gamble what's left, finish what my father started?'

'Not gamble, invest.'

'Meanwhile I'm what? A performing earl, the public face of Hawksley, like some medieval lord of the manor...'

'You are the lord of the manor.'

'It's all about publicity with you, isn't it? You say you don't want it but you can't see any way but the obvious—photos and newspapers and the public.'

'No.' She was on her feet. 'But with a place like Hawksley the right kind of publicity is a blessing.'

'There is no such thing as the right publicity.'

She stared at him. 'Come on, Seb, you know that's not true. Look at your books!'

'They're work, this is my home.' His voice was tight.

Daisy bit her lip, her eyes troubled. 'You can't see past your fears. You are so determined to do things your way you won't even consider any alternatives!'

His mouth curled in disgust. 'Is this about those damned TV lectures?'

'They would be a great start.'

Bitterness coated his mouth. 'I thought you understood.'

'I do. But you want me to marry you, to give you an heir. An heir to what? To worry? To debt? To fear? Or to a thriving business and a home with history—and a roof that doesn't leak?'

He pushed his chair back and stumbled to his

feet. 'Hawksley is mine, Daisy. Mine! I will sort this out and make it right.'

Her eyes were huge. 'I don't get any say?'

That wasn't what he meant and she knew it. 'Stop twisting my words and stop creating drama.'

But she wasn't backing down. He didn't know her eyes could burn so brightly. 'You can't just shut me down, Seb, every time we have a difference of opinion. That's not how life works, not how marriage works.'

'I'm not shutting you down.' He just didn't want to argue. What was wrong with that?

'You are! If we are going to do this then we have to be partners. I have to be able to contribute without you accusing me of picking fights. I have to be involved in your decisions and your life.'

He couldn't answer, didn't know what to say. He hadn't expected her to push him like this. He had underestimated her, that was clear. What had he expected? A compliant partner, someone to warm his bed and agree with him?

He could feel his heart speeding up, his palms slick with sweat. He had obviously overestimated himself just as much. Pompous ass that he was.

'That's not what you want, is it?' Her voice was just a whisper. 'You're happy for me to redecorate some rooms but you don't want my input, not where it matters.' Her voice broke. 'You're right, what does a romantically inclined girl with no qualifications know anyway?'

'That's not what I said.'

'It's what you think though.'

He couldn't deny it.

The blue eyes were swimming. 'I know I said I could do this, Seb, but I'm not sure I'm the kind of woman who can warm your bed and raise your children and not be needed in your life.'

She could read him like a book. He wanted to say that he did need her but the words wouldn't come. 'You promised to try.'

'I have tried.' Her cry sounded torn from the heart. Half of him wanted to step forward and enfold her in his arms, promise her that it would be okay—the other half of him recoiled from the sheer emotion.

'So what are you saying? The wedding is off?'

She swallowed. 'I don't know. I know how important getting married is for the baby's sake but I have to think about me as well. I need some time, Seb. Some time on my own to figure things out. I'm sorry.'

And while he was still searching for the right

words, the right sentiments, a way to make her stay she slipped out of the room and he knew that he'd lost her.

And he had no idea how to find her again.

CHAPTER ELEVEN

SHE'D LEFT HER favourite camera at Hawksley. She'd also left her favourite laptop and half of her hats but right now it was her camera she needed.

If she wasn't going to expose herself to her own merciless gaze then she needed to turn that gaze elsewhere. She needed to find a subject and lose herself in it.

Daisy stared mindlessly out of the windscreen. She had other cameras at her studio but returning there, right now, felt like a retreat. Worse, it felt like an admission of failure.

But she had failed, hadn't she?

She'd tried to change the rules.

They hadn't even managed the shotgun marriage part before she had started interfering. Demanding responses, pushing him, putting together PowerPoint presentations. Daisy leaned forward until her forehead knocked against the steering wheel.

She was a fool.

And yet…

Slowly Daisy straightened, her hands pressing tighter on the wheel. And yet she had felt more right than she had in a long, long time. As if she had finally burst out of her chrysalis.

She didn't know if she could willingly shut herself back in. She'd enjoyed the research, enjoyed finding conclusions—she'd even enjoyed figuring out PowerPoint in the end after she had emerged victorious after the first few scuffles. She'd never put together any kind of business plan before, never pushed herself.

Never allowed herself to broaden her horizons, to think she might be capable of achieving more. Hidden behind her camera just as Seb hid behind his qualifications.

She'd wanted to help him. Had seen how much he was struggling, torn between his career and his home, the expectations of his past and the worries of the present.

But he didn't want her help. Didn't need her.

Without conscious thought, just following her instinct, Daisy began to drive, following the road signs on autopilot until she turned down the long lane that led to her childhood home. She pulled the small car to a stop and turned off the engine, relief seeping through her bones. This was where she needed to be, right now.

It had been a long time since she had run home with her problems.

It was only a short walk along the lane and through the gates that led to the hall but with each step Daisy's burden lightened, just a little. Maybe asking for help wasn't a sign of weakness.

Maybe it was maturity.

Huntingdon Hall glowed a soft gold in the late afternoon light. Daisy paused, taking in its graceful lines, the long rows of windows, the perfectly symmetrical wings, the well-maintained and prosperous air of the house. It wasn't just smaller than Hawksley, newer than half of Hawksley—it was a family home. Loved, well cared for and welcoming.

But it wasn't her home any more, hadn't been for a long time. She shut her eyes for a moment, visualising the way the sun lit up the Norman keep, the thousand-year-old tower reflected in the water. When had Hawksley begun to feel like *her* home?

The kitchen doors stood ajar and she ran up the steps, inhaling gratefully the familiar scent of fresh flowers, beeswax and the spicy vanilla scent her mother favoured. Inside the kitchen was as immaculate as always, a huge open-plan cooking, eating and relaxing space, the back wall floor-to-ceiling glass doors bringing the outside inside no matter what the weather.

She'd walked away from all this comfort, luxury and love at eighteen so convinced she wouldn't be able to find herself here, convinced she was the family joke, the family outcast. Tears burned the backs of her eyes as she looked at the vast array of photographs hung on the walls; not her father's record covers or her mother's most famous shoots but the girls from bald, red-faced babies, through gap-toothed childhood to now. Interspersed and lovingly framed were some of Daisy's own photos including her degree shoot prints.

What must it have cost them to let her go? To allow her the freedom to make her own mistakes?

'Hey, Daisy girl.' Her father's rich American drawl remained unchanged despite three decades living in the UK. 'Is your mother with you?' He looked round for his wife, hope and affection lighting up his face. What must it be like, Daisy wondered with a wistful envy, to love someone else so much that your first thought was always of them?

'Nope, she's still browbeating the caterers and

obsessing over hairstyles.' She leant gratefully into her father's skinny frame as he pulled her into a cuddle. How long was it since she had allowed herself to be held like this? For too long she had stopped after a peck and a squeeze of the shoulders. 'Hi, Dad.'

'It's good to see you, Daisy girl.' He pulled back to look her over, a frown furrowing the famously craggy face. 'You look exhausted. Your mother working you too hard?'

'I think you and Mum had the right idea running away.' Daisy tried not to wriggle away from his scrutiny.

'It saved a lot of bother,' he agreed, but the keen eyes were full of concern. 'Drink?'

'Just water, please.' She accepted the ice-cold glass gratefully, carrying it over to the comfortable cluster of sofas grouped around the windows, sinking onto one with a sigh of relief.

She had begun to recreate this feeling in the kitchen at Hawksley, sanding back the old kitchen cupboards so that they could be repainted a soft grey and bringing in one of the better sofas from an unused salon to curl up on by the Aga. Slowly, step by step turning the few rooms she and Seb used into warm, comfortable places. Into a family home.

'I feel like I should be coming to you with words of advice and wisdom.' Rick sat down on the sofa opposite, a bottle of beer in one hand. 'After three daughters and three decades of marriage you'd think I'd know something. But all I know is don't go to bed angry, wake up counting your blessings and always try and see the other person's point of view. If you can manage that—' he raised his bottle to her '—then you should be okay.'

'Funny.' She smiled at him. 'Mum said something very similar.'

Rick took a swig of his beer. 'Well, your mother's a wise woman.'

Daisy swung her legs up onto the sofa, reclining against the solid arm and letting the cushions enfold her. She half closed her eyes, allowing the sounds and smells of her childhood home to comfort her. After a few moments Rick got up and she could hear him clattering about in the food preparation part of the kitchen. Her eyelids fluttered shut and she allowed herself to fall into a doze, feeling safe for the first time in a long while.

'Here you go.' She roused as a plate was set before her. 'I know it's fashionable for brides to waste away before their wedding but if you get any thinner, Daisy girl, I'll be having to hold you down as we walk down that aisle.'

'My favourite.' The all-too-ready tears pricked her eyelids as Daisy looked at the plate holding a grilled cheese and tomato sandwich and a bowl of tomato soup. Her childhood comfort food— not coincidentally also the limit of Rick Cross's cooking skills. 'Thanks, Dad.'

Her father didn't say another word while she ate; instead he picked up one of the seemingly endless supplies of guitars that lay in every room of the house and began to strum some chords. It had used to drive Daisy mad, his inability to stay quiet and still, but now she appreciated it for what it was. A safety blanket, just like her camera.

As always the slightly stodgy mix of white bread, melted cheese and sweet tomatoes slipped down easily and a full stomach made her feel in-finitely better. Rick continued to strum as Daisy carried her empty dishes to the sink, the chords turning into a well-known marching song.

Rick began to croon the lyrics in the throaty tones that had made him a star. He looked up at his daughter, a twinkle in his eyes. 'Thought I might sing this instead of making a speech.'

She couldn't do it, couldn't lie to him a single moment longer. So she would slip back into being the problem daughter, the mistake-making disaster zone. Maybe she deserved it.

She could take it. She had to take it.

She was tired of doing it all alone. Tired of shutting her family out. Tired of always being strong, of putting her need to be independent before her family.

Maybe *this* was what being a grown-up meant. Not shutting yourself away but knowing when it was okay to accept help. When it was okay to lean on someone else. The day Seb had come to help her with the wedding had been one of the best days of her adult life. She'd come so close to relying on him.

Tension twisted her stomach as she fought to find the right words. But there were no right words. Just the facts.

Daisy turned, looked him straight in the eyes and readied herself. 'I'm pregnant. Dad, I'm pregnant and I don't know what to do.'

Her father didn't react straight away. His fingers fell off the guitar and he carefully put the instrument to one side, his face shuttered. Slowly he got to his feet, walking over to Daisy before pulling her in close, holding her as if he meant to never let her go.

The skinny shoulders were stronger than they looked. Daisy allowed herself to lean against them, to let her father bear her weight and finally, finally stopped fighting the tears she had swallowed back for so long, shudders shaking her whole body as the sobs tore out of her.

'It's okay, Daisy girl,' her father crooned, stroking her hair as if she were still his little girl. 'It's okay.'

But she couldn't stop, not yet, even though the great gusty sobs had turned into hiccups and the tears had soaked her father's shirt right through. The relief of finally not having to put on a brave face was too much and it was several minutes before her father could escort her back to the sofa, setting another glass of water and several tissues in front of her.

'Hold on,' he said. 'If living with a pack of women has taught me anything it's that there's a surefire remedy for this kind of situation.' He walked, with the catlike grace that made him such a hypnotic stage performer, to the fridge and, opening the freezer door, extracted a pint of ice cream. 'Here you go, Daisy girl,' he said, setting it down in front of her and handing her a spoon. 'Dig in.'

He didn't say anything for a while. Just sat there as Daisy scooped the creamy cold chocolatey goodness out of the carton, allowing it to melt on her tongue. She couldn't manage more than a couple of mouthfuls, the gesture of far more comfort than the actual ice cream.

'I take it this wasn't planned?' His voice was calm, completely non-judgemental.

Daisy shook her head. 'No.'

'How long have you known?'

She could feel the colour creeping over her cheeks, couldn't meet her father's eye. 'A month. I told Seb three weeks ago.'

'This is why you're getting married?'

Daisy nodded. 'It's because of Hawksley, and the title. If the baby isn't legitimate…' Her voice trailed off.

'Crazy Brits.' Her dad sat back. 'Do you love him, Daisy girl?'

Did she what? She liked him—sometimes. Desired him for sure. The way his hair fell over his forehead, a little too long and messy for fashion. The clear green of his eyes, the way they darkened with emotion. The lean strength of him, unexpected in an academic. The way he listened to her, asked her questions, respected her, made her feel that maybe she had something to contribute—until today.

She understood him, knew why he strived so hard to excel in everything he did, tried to keep himself aloof, the fear of being judged.

Her father's gaze intensified. 'It's not that hard a question, Daisy girl. When you know, you know.'

'Yes.' The knowledge hit her hard, almost winding her. 'Yes, I do. But he doesn't love me and that's why I don't know if I can do it. I don't know if I can marry him. If I can say those words to someone who doesn't want to hear them, for him to say them to me and not mean them.' That was it, she realised with a sharp clarity. She had been prepared to lie to everyone but she couldn't bear for him to lie to her. To make promises he didn't mean.

'Love means that much to you?' Her father's eyes were kind, knowing.

Daisy put her hand down to cradle her still-flat stomach. She wanted the baby; she already loved it. Which love meant more? Pulled at her more? What was worse? Depriving her baby of its heritage or bringing it up in an unequal, unhappy household?

'With your example before me? Of course it does. I want a husband who looks at me the way you look at Mum. That's what I've always wanted. But it's not just about me, not any more. Oh, Dad, what am I going to do?'

Her father put an arm around her and she sank into his embrace wishing for one moment that she were a little girl again and that there was nothing her dad couldn't fix. 'That's up to you, Daisy girl. Only you can decide. But we're all here for you, whatever happens. Remember that, darling. I know how independent you are but we're here. You're not alone.'

Loneliness had been such a constant friend for so many years he had barely noticed it leave.

Yet now it had returned it felt heavier than ever.

The primroses carpeted the woodland floor, their pale beauty a vivid reminder of the colour overtaking his home. Sherry liked a theme and had incorporated the yellow-and-white colour scheme into everything from the guest towels to the bunting already hung in the marquee. It was like living in a giant egg.

Apart from the rooms Daisy had been working on. She had kept her mother out of those, keeping them private, personal.

Creating a family space.

His throat closed tight. *Their* family space.

Normally Seb loved this time of year, watching the world bud, shaking off the sleepy austerity of winter. It wasn't as obvious in Oxford as it was here at Hawksley where every day signalled something new.

Oxford. It had been his focus for so long, his sole goal. To excel in his field. He had almost made it.

But suddenly it didn't seem that important, more like a remembered dream than a passion. His research? Yes. Digging into the past, feeling it come alive, transcribing it for a modern audience, that he missed. But college politics, hungover undergraduates, teaching, tourist-filled streets, the buzz of the city?

Seb breathed in the revelation. He didn't miss it at all.

He was home. This was where he belonged.

But not alone. He had been alone long enough.

Seb retraced his steps, anticipating the moment his steps would lead him out of the wood and over the hill, that first glimpse of Hawksley Castle standing, majestic, by the lake edge. The Norman keep, grey, watchful, looking out over the water flanked by the white plaster and timbered Tudor hall, picturesque with the light reflected off the lead-paned windows. Finally the house itself, a perfect example of neoclassical Georgian architecture.

Daisy was right: it would make a wonderful setting for a TV series.

Seb's heart twisted. Painfully.

What if she didn't come back? How would he explain her absence to her mother? The guests already beginning to arrive in the village and in neighbouring hotels? If the wedding was called off the resulting publicity would be incredible, every detail of his own parents' doomed marriage exhumed and re-examined over and over.

The usual nausea swirled, sweat beading at his forehead, but it wasn't at the prospect of the screaming headlines and taunting comments. No, Seb realised. It was at the thought of the wedding being called off.

Slowly he wandered back towards the castle barely noticing the spring sunshine warming his shoulders. No wedding. It wasn't as if he had wanted this grand, showy affair anyway. It was a compromise he had had to make for the baby, wasn't it?

Or was it?

The truth was he hadn't hesitated. He'd taken one look at Daisy's face as she'd read through that long list of names and known he couldn't deny her the wedding of her dreams.

Truth was he couldn't deny her anything.

He wanted to give her everything—not that she'd take it, absurdly proud as she was.

She was hardworking, earnest and underestimated herself so much she allowed everybody else to underestimate her too, hiding behind her red lipstick, her quirky style and her camera.

He knew how she put herself down, made light of her own perceived failures, preempting the judgement she was sure would come. What must it have taken to put that presentation together, to show him her work—and yet he had thrown all her enthusiasm, all her help back in her face.

Shame washed over him, hot and tight. He hadn't wanted to listen, to accept that a fresh pair of eyes could ever see anything in Hawksley that he couldn't see. Hadn't wanted to accept that he was stuck on the wrong path.

He had spent so long ensuring he was nothing like his spoilt, immoral parents he had turned himself into his grandfather: upstanding sure, also rigid, a relic from a time long dead, refusing to accept the world had changed even as his staff and income shrank and his bills multiplied.

It seemed a long way back to the castle, weighted down with guilt and shame. The truth was Daisy was right: he did need to make some changes and fast.

Starting with the estate. Much as he wanted to jump in his car, find her, beg her forgiveness he had to make the much-needed changes first. That way he could show her.

Show her that he had listened, show her that her work had value.

That he valued her.

Seb stood still, feeling his heart beat impossibly hard, impossibly loud.

Was this valuing her? This nausea, this knot of worry, this urge to do whatever it took to show her?

Or was it something more? Was it love?

It was messy and painful, just as he had feared, but it was more than that.

It was miraculous.

She made him a better person. It was up to him to repay that gift, even though it would take him the rest of his life.

The estate office was, as usual, a mess, cold and cluttered, an unattractive tangle of paperwork, old furniture, tools and filing cabinets. It felt unloved, impermanent. Seb sank down into the creaking old office chair and looked about at the utilitarian shelves, filled with broken bits of machinery and rusting tools. This was no way to run a place the size of Hawksley.

He picked up a notebook and flipped it open to a fresh white page. It mocked him with the unwritten possibilities and he sat for a moment, paralysed by how much he had to do, how sweeping the changes ahead.

But this wasn't about him, not any more. It was about his child, about his heritage, about the man he was—and the man he should be.

It was about his future wife.

The first thing he needed to do was admit he needed some help, he couldn't do it all on his own no matter how much he wanted to.

He uncapped his fountain pen and began to write.

1. Resign from college

Seb sat back and looked at the words, waited to feel sad, resentful, to feel the weight of failure. He still had so much more to achieve; the visiting professorship at Harvard for one. Was he ready to give up his academic career? He could produce another ten bestselling books but without his college credentials they would mean nothing, not to his colleagues.

But the expected emotions didn't materialise; instead the burden on his shoulders lessened.

He leant forward again.

2. Employ a professional estate manager

Daisy was right, damn her. What use was he to anyone, sitting up late, scrutinising crop-rotation plans and cattle lists? He had done his best but he still knew less than an apprentice cattle man. If he put in an estate manager he could free his time up for writing—and for the house itself. Which led to the third thing. Admitting that Hawksley wasn't just his family home, it was a living legacy and he needed to start treating it as such.

*3. Tidy and redecorate the offices to a profes-
sional standard*

So that he could then…

4. Employ an events planner

*5. Talk to the solicitor about breaking into the
trust and investing in the estate*

What was it Daisy had suggested? An internal
structure in the Norman keep. That could work,
maintain the integrity of the historical ruins while
making it both safe and comfortable for weddings and parties. Seb winced. It looked as if the
medieval-themed banquets might be unavoidable
after all. As long as he wasn't expected to wear
tights and a jerkin…

What else? Holiday cottages, nature trails… He
thought back. It had only been this morning. How
was it possible that so few hours had passed? She
had left her laptop behind. He needed to take a
look, see what other ideas he had dismissed. But
there was definitely one more thing to add to the
list.

*6. Tell my agent I am willing to consider
TV ideas*

* * *

Her room looked just as it always did, with no inkling that its mistress had fled. The usual jumble of scarves, the ever-increasing collection of hats. Seb stood at the door and inhaled the faint floral scent she always wore.

When had he begun to associate that smell with home?

He didn't want her hidden away behind the discreet door, not any more. He wanted her with him; hats, scarves and whatever else she needed to make herself at home. Her rooms would make an incredible nursery.

If she would just come back.

He stepped past the neatly made bed and into the small chamber Daisy used as an office. Her laptop still stood open and, when he tentatively touched a key, it lit up, her PowerPoint presentation still on the screen. Seb took it back to the beginning and began to read.

Shame flared again. Searing as he flicked through the slides. She had put a lot of time into this. For him. She had only looked at comparable estates in terms of size and had got as much useful information as she could including entrance prices, numbers of staff, opening hours and affiliations to member organisations. It was invaluable data, the beginnings of a business plan right here.

He closed the file down and sat back, his chest tight. How could he make it up to her?

Seb was about to switch the laptop off when a file caught his eye. Saved to her desktop, it was simply titled Hawksley. Was it more research? Curious, he double clicked.

More photos. Of course. A smile curved his mouth as he looked at his beloved home from Daisy's perspective: panoramic views, detailed close-ups, the volunteers at work, the farms. All the myriad details that made up Hawksley chronicled. She understood it as much as he did—possibly even more. She was so much more than the mother of his child, more than a fitting mistress for this huge, complicated and much-loved house.

She was perfect.

Another photo flashed up, black and white, grainy, an almost-sepia filter. It was Seb, sitting at his desk. His first instinct was to recoil, the way he always did when faced with a candid shot, the familiar churn of horror, of violation.

But then he looked again. He was reading, his forehead furrowed; he looked tired, a little stressed. It completely encapsulated the past few months, the toil they had taken on him.

Another image, Seb again, this one in full colour. He was outside, leaning against a tractor chatting to one of the tenant farmers. This time he looked relaxed, happy.

Another—Seb in Oxford, mid flow, gesticulating, eyes shining as he spoke. Another, another, another…

It wasn't just Hawksley she understood, had got to the heart of. It was Seb himself.

He closed the laptop lid and sat back, images whirling about his brain. Not the ones she had captured but those images firmly stuck in his memory. The tall, earnest girl stuck in the snow, desperate to fulfil her promise to a couple she didn't even know. That same girl later that night, eyes half closed in ecstasy, her long limbs wrapped around him.

The look in her eyes when she told him she was pregnant. Her reaction to his proposal. Her desperate plea for him to pretend he loved her. Her need to be loved. Wanted. Appreciated.

Did he love her enough? Want her enough? Appreciate her enough?

Did he deserve her?

Seb's hands curled into fists. He liked having her here. He liked waking up next to her, liked listening to her take on life, liked the way she brought fresh air and life into his ancient home.

He liked the way she used her camera as a shield, he liked how hard she worked, how seriously she took each and every wedding. He liked the way she focused in on the tiniest detail and made it special.

How she made him feel special.

He liked her dress sense, the vivid shade of red lipstick. He liked how long it took her to choose the hat of the day, how that hat evoked her mood. He liked her first thing in the morning, rosy-cheeked, make-up free, hair tousled.

He liked pretty much everything about her. He loved her.

They were supposed to be getting married in just a few days. Married. For him a business arrangement sealed with a soulless diamond solitaire. He was a fool.

He flipped open her laptop again, clicking onto her email. He needed her sister Rose's email address. Maybe, just maybe, he could put this right. It might not be too late for him after all.

And then he would bring her home.

CHAPTER TWELVE

'Hɪ.'

It seemed such an inadequate word. Daisy's breath hitched as Seb came to a stop and looked at her. He was pale, his eyes looked bruised as if he hadn't slept at all and a small, shameful thrill of victory throbbed through her.

Only to ebb with the realisation that it probably wasn't Daisy herself he had spent the night tossing and turning over. The publicity that calling the wedding off would cause? Probably. Losing a legitimate heir? Most definitely.

'Hello.'

He took a step forward and stopped, as if she were a wild animal who might bolt.

It was chillier today and Daisy wrapped her arms around herself, inadequate protection against the sharp breeze blowing across the lawn.

'How did you know I was here?' Had her father called him?

'I didn't. I tried the studio first.'

That meant what? Three hours of driving? A small, unwanted shot of hope pulsed through her. 'I'm sorry for just taking off. I know how much you hate emotional scenes but I really needed some space.'

'I understand.' He swallowed, and her eyes were drawn to the strong lines of his throat. 'I've been thinking myself.'

'About what?'

'Us. Hawksley. My parents. My job. Everything really.'

'That's a lot of thinking.'

'Yes.' His mouth quirked. Daisy tried to look away but she couldn't, her eyes drawn to the firm lines of his jaw, the shape of his mouth.

'Does my mother know why I left?' Sherry had been sleeping at the castle the past week, dedicating every hour to her daughter's wedding. How could Daisy tell her it was all for nothing?

'No. I just said you needed some space,' His eyes were fixed on her with a painful intensity; she was stripped under his gaze. 'She and Violet have gone to your studio to decorate.'

'To what?' What day was it? Her stomach dropped at the realisation. 'Oh, no, the hen night. It's supposed to be low-key.'

'I got the sense that things may have evolved a little. Violet was very excited about buying in some special straws?'

'Straws?'

'Shaped straws…anatomically shaped straws.'

'Oh. Oh! Really? Vi has?'

'I didn't want to tell them they may not be needed, not until I'd spoken to you.' His mouth curved into the familiar half smile and Daisy had to curl her fingers into a fist to stop herself from reaching out to trace its line. 'And, well, it's always good to have a stock of penis straws in.'

'I'll bear that in mind.'

All the things she had planned to say to him had gone clear out of her mind. Daisy had been rehearsing speeches all night but in the end it was her father's words that echoed round and round in her mind. *When you know, you know.*

She knew she loved him. Just one look at him and she was weakening, wanted to hold him, feel his arms around her, allow him to kiss away her fears. But he wouldn't do that, would he? No. Kisses were strictly for the bedroom.

And wonderfully, toe-curlingly delicious as they were, that wasn't enough.

'Seb,' she began.

Another step and he was right before her. 'No hat.' His hand reached out and smoothed down her hair. 'No lipstick.' He ran it down the side of her cheek, drawing one finger along her bottom lip. Daisy's mouth parted at the caress, the tingle of his touch shivering through her.

'I didn't bring anything with me.' She had raided Violet's wardrobe first thing: jeans, a long-sleeved T-shirt. Ordinary, sensible clothes. She felt naked in them; there was nothing to hide behind.

'You're beautiful whatever you wear.' His voice was husky and her knees weakened as she looked up and saw the heat in his eyes.

Her mouth dried. All she wanted to do was press her mouth to his, forget herself, forget the wedding, the baby, her doubts in the surety of his kiss. 'I can't.' She put a hand out, warding him off.

'Daisy.' He swallowed and she steeled herself. Steeled herself against any entreaty. Steeled herself against the knowledge that whatever he told her, however he tried to convince her there were words he would never say no matter how much she yearned to hear them.

And steeled herself not to yield regardless.

'Will you come back with me? No—' As she

began to shake her head. 'I don't mean for good. I mean now. There's something I want to show you.'

So much for all her good intentions. But she had to return at some point didn't she? To collect her things. To help dismantle the wedding her mother had spent three weeks lovingly putting together.

To start forgetting the jolt her heart gave as the car pulled over the hill and she saw Hawksley, proud in the distance.

Or to make up her mind to make the best of it, to keep her word, to put their baby first. Trouble was she still didn't know which way to turn.

To be true to her own heart or to be true to her child?

And in the end weren't they the same thing?

Daisy started walking, no destination in mind; she just had to keep moving. Seb fell into step beside her, not touching her, the inches between them a chasm as she rounded the corner past the stables.

'I was thinking that this end stable would make a great studio. They're not listed so you could do whatever you wanted for light—glass walls, anything. I know you want to carry on photographing weddings and that's fine but if you did want to exhibit your other work we could even add a gallery.'

Was this what he wanted to show her? A way of making her career more acceptable? Her heart plummeted. 'A gallery?'

'Only if you wanted to. I know how much you love weddings, but your other work is amazing too. It's up to you.'

'It would make a great space, it's just...' She faltered, unable to find the words.

'It's just an idea. This is your home too, Daisy. I just want you to know that I can support you too, whatever you need. The way you support me.' He sounded sincere enough.

Yesterday those words might even have been enough.

Her heart was so heavy it felt as if it had fallen out of her chest, shrivelled into a stone in the pit of her stomach. She had to keep moving, had to try and figure out the right thing to say. The right thing to do.

The marquee had been set up at the far end of the courtyard and curiosity pulled her there; she hadn't seen inside since it had been decorated.

'Wow.' Swathes of yellow and silk covered the ceiling, creating an exotic canopy over the hardwood dance floor. Buffet tables were set up at one end, covered in yellow cloths, and benches were set around the edges.

Daisy swivelled and walked back through the tent, trying to envision it full, to see it as it would be in just forty-eight hours filled with laughter and dancing—or would it be taken down unused?

A canvas canopy connected the marquee with the door to the Great Hall, a precaution against a rainy day. The heavy oak doors were open and she stepped through them, Seb still at her side. 'Oh,' she said softly as she looked around. 'Oh, it's beautiful.'

Daisy had seen the Great Hall in several guises. Empty save for the weight of history in each of the carved panels, the huge old oak beams. Set up for another wedding ceremony and, later, a busy party venue. Her mother's workspace complete with whiteboards, elaborate floorplans and fore-lock-tugging minions.

But she had never seen it look as it did today.

The dais at the far end was simply furnished with a white desk and chairs for the registrar, flanked on both sides by tall white urns filled with Violet's unmistakeable flower arrangements: classy, elegant yet with a uniquely modern twist.

A heavy tapestry hung from the back wall: Seb's coat of arms.

Facing the dais were rows of chairs, all covered in white, hand-sewn fabric daisy chains wound around their legs and backs.

A yellow carpet lay along the aisle ready for her to walk up, and more of the intricate woven daisy chains hung from the great beams.

'Mum has worked so hard,' she breathed.

'The poor staff have done three dummy runs to make sure they can get the tables set up perfectly in the hour and a half your mother has allowed for drinks, canapés and photographs—on the lawn if dry and warm enough, in the marquee if not. Everything is stacked in the back in perfect order—linens, table decorations, place settings, crockery. Your mother should really run the country,' Seb added, his mouth twisting into a half smile. 'Her organisational skills and, ah, persuasive skills are extraordinary.'

'We've always said that.' Daisy stared at the room perfectly set up for the perfect wedding. For her perfect wedding.

This was what she had always wanted—she had just never known who would be standing by her side. She had certainly never imagined a tall, slightly scruffy academic with penetrating green eyes, too-long dark hair and a title dating back four centuries.

Could she imagine it now? Standing up there making promises to Seb? Images swirled round and round, memories of the last three weeks: tender moments, passionate moments—and that remote, curt aloofness of his. Nausea rose as a stabbing pain shot through her temples; she swayed and he leapt forward, one arm around her shoulders, guiding her to a chair.

Daisy rubbed her head, willing the pain away. 'I'm okay. I forgot to eat breakfast.'

'Come with me, there's some croissants in the kitchen. And there's something I want to show you.'

The knot in her stomach was too big, too tight, food an impossibility until she spoke to him. But would a few more minutes of pretending that all this could be hers hurt?

'I told you I had been doing a lot of thinking,' he said as they stepped back into the courtyard. The wind was still sharp but the sun had come out, slanting through the grey clouds, shining onto the golden stone of the main house. Seb had a glimpse of a future, of children running in and out of the door, games in the courtyard, dens in the wood.

If he could just convince her to stay.

'I've resigned from the university.'

She came to an abrupt stop. 'You've what?'

'Resigned. I'll still write, of course. In fact, without my academic commitments I'll have more time to write, more time to explore other periods, other stories.'

'Why?'

'I'm needed here.' But that wasn't all of it. 'I love delving into the past, you know that. And I loved academia too. Because it was safe, there were rules. When I was a boy—' he inhaled, steady against the rush of memories '—I just wanted to keep my head down, to do the right thing. At school, as long as you worked hard, played hard and didn't tell tales then life was easy. I liked that. It was safe compared to the turbulence of my parents' existence. In a way I guess I never left school. Straight to university and then on an academic path. Everything was clear, easy. I knew exactly what I had to do, what was expected of me—until I inherited Hawksley.

'Until I met you.'

A quiver passed through her but she didn't speak

as they walked around the house and in through the main door, towards the library, their steps in harmony. He pushed the library door open and stood there, in the entrance.

'I've made some other decisions too. I've spoken to my agent and asked her to investigate TV work, I've got an agency looking for suitable candidates to take over the estate management and kick-start an events programme and I've asked three architects to submit plans for converting the outbuildings.'

She did speak then, her voice soft. 'You've been very busy.'

'No.' He shook his head. 'I've been at a standstill. You were the one who was busy, busy looking into the future. I've just taken your ideas and made the next step. But I don't want to do it alone.'

She shook her head, tears swimming in her eyes. Tears were good, right? They meant she felt something. Meant she cared.

He needed to throw everything he had at her. Strip away the diffidence and fear and lay it all out. No matter how much it cost him to do it, the alternative was much worse.

'Daisy, I do need you. Not just physically, although my bed has been so empty the last two nights I couldn't sleep. But I need you to challenge me, to push me, to make me take my head out of the sand and face the future.'

'You'd have got there on your own, eventually.' Would he? He doubted it.

'Seb, I can't live in fear. I don't like being in the papers but I accept it may happen. I can't hide just in case some bored person snaps me. And I can't not say what I think because you don't like emotional outbursts. Life isn't that tidy.'

'I thought it could be,' he admitted. 'I didn't see a middle way between the hysterical ups and downs of my parents' life and the formality of my grandparents. If it was a choice between sitting at opposite sides of a fifteen-foot table and making polite conversation or throwing plates and screaming then give me cold soup and a hoarse voice any day.'

'Most families aren't so extreme…'

'No. No, they're not. And I don't want either of those for the baby. I want it to grow up like you did, part of a happy, stable family. With two parents who love each other.'

Her eyes fell but not before he saw the hurt blaze in them. 'You don't have to say that. I don't want you to lie to make me feel better.'

'The only person I've been lying to was myself.' Seb took her chin and tilted it, trying to make her see the sincerity in his eyes.

'Love, it's complicated. It's messy and emotional and difficult. I wasn't ready for it. But then you came sauntering in with your hats and that mouth—' his eyes dropped to her mouth, lush and full even without its usual coating of slick red '—your camera and your absolute belief in love. Your belief in me and in Hawksley and you turned my world upside down. And not just because of the baby.'

Her eyes blazed blue with hope. 'Really?'

'I hadn't been able to stop thinking of you since that first night,' he told her frankly. It was all or nothing time. 'I asked the groom who you were the next morning and he sent me a link to your website. I must have clicked onto the contact me button a dozen times. But I was afraid. Nobody had ever got under my skin like that before. And then you came back…'

She laughed softly. 'You looked like you'd seen a ghost.'

Seb smiled back down at her, the warmth creeping back into her voice giving him a jolt of hope. 'I couldn't believe my luck. But I was terrified too.

Of how you made me feel. How much I wanted you. There was nothing sensible about that. And the more I got to know you, Daisy, the more terrified I was.'

'I'm that scary?' A light had begun to shine in her eyes, the full mouth quivering.

'You are quite frankly the most terrifying woman I have ever met—and I am including your mother in that. And if you ever begin to believe in yourself, Daisy Huntingdon-Cross, then I don't think there is anything you won't achieve. Because—' he moved in slightly closer, emboldened by the curve of her smile '—you are definitely the smartest out of the two of us. It took you leaving for me to acknowledge how I felt about you. But now that I have I want to tell you every day. Every hour of every day. I love you, Daisy, and I really, really hope that you will marry me in two days.'

With those words the load he had been carrying for so long, the fear, the shame, finally broke free. Whatever her answer he would always be grateful to her for that—even if he had to spend the rest of his life proving the truth of his words to her.

'You love me? You think I'm smart?' Her voice broke and he dropped her chin to encircle her waist, pulling her in close. He inhaled the soft floral scent of her hair. It was like coming home.

'Ridiculously so.' Reluctantly he let her go, backing into the half-open door and pushing it open, taking her hand and pulling her inside.

'You're not the only one to see that the house needs changing, needs making into a home. I can't begin to match what you've achieved but I'm trying to make a start.'

Daisy stood stock-still, staring at the wall. Gone was the line of stern portraits; no more bewigged gentleman with terrifying eyebrows or stern Victorians with bristling moustaches. Even Seb's grandfather had been removed to a more fitting place in the long gallery.

Instead two huge canvas prints hung on the wall, surrounded by smaller black-and-white prints of Hawksley: the castle, the woods, the gardens. Her photos.

She looked up at the photos, eyes widening as she took in the photo of Seb. It was the one she'd taken of him in Oxford, the light behind him. It felt hubristic having such a large picture of himself on his own wall.

But it wasn't just his wall now.

Flanking him was another black-and-white

photo, this time of Daisy—also at work. The trees framed her as she held the camera up to her face, her profile intent, her focus absolute.

'Where…?' She gaped up at the picture. 'Where on earth did you get that?'

'I took it.' Seb tried and failed to keep the pride out of his voice. 'I had a moment in between those photobooth shots and I turned around—and there you were. Lost in the moment. So I snapped it. I saved it onto my computer, thought you might want it for your website or something.'

'It's actually pretty good, nice composition.'

'Total and utter fluke,' he admitted. 'Daisy—' he took her hands in his '—I want the castle, every room, every decision we make to be about us. About you, me and the baby. I want to help you turn Hawksley into a family home. Into a house full of love and laughter. I asked you to marry me three weeks ago for all sorts of sensible reasons. I told you marriage was a business. I was a fool.

'I want to marry you because I love you and I hope you love me. Because I actually don't think I can live without you—and I know I can't survive without you. So, Daisy.' Seb let go of her hands and took out the ring. The ring that had miraculously arrived by overnight courier, the ring that Daisy's sister had somehow known to have ready.

Slowly, looking up into her face, he lowered himself onto one knee.

'Daisy Huntingdon-Cross. Will you please, please marry me?'

'Get up!' Daisy pulled him up, snaking her arms around his neck, smiling up at him, her eyes full of joy. 'Well, the guests *are* already invited.'

'They are.'

'It would be a shame to waste my mother's hard work.'

'A real shame.'

'And the chance to see my mother with a penis straw is not one to be passed up.'

Seb grimaced. 'I can personally live without that image, my love. But knock yourself out.'

'Say that again.'

'Knock yourself out?'

'No, the name you called me.'

'My love.' Seb's heart felt as if it might explode from his chest as he bent his head, ready to capture her mouth with his. 'My love.'

EPILOGUE

'READY, DAISY GIRL?'

Daisy pulled at the waist of her dress with nervous fingers before smiling up at her father.

'Ready, Dad.'

'Well, I'm not.' Rick Cross's eyes were suspiciously damp. 'I don't think I will ever be ready to walk you down that aisle and hand you over to another man.'

Violet rolled her eyes. 'It's the twenty-first century, Dad. Nobody gets handed over.'

'If anyone is in charge in this house, I'm sorry, I mean in this castle, it's Daisy. I've only been here a few hours and even I can see she's got that poor earl right under her thumb.'

Daisy stuck her tongue out at Rose. 'How I wish I had made you wear frills.'

Her sisters looked stunning in the simple silk dresses she had chosen. The sweetheart necklines and ruched bodices were white, flaring out into yellow knee-length skirts. Her dress had a similar bodice although instead of bare shoulders, hers were covered with a sheer lace and her floor-length skirt fell straight from the bust in a sweep of white silk to the floor.

'And I wish I had made that ring too large.' Rose nodded at the band made of twisted yellow gold, white gold petals alternating with small diamonds that adorned Daisy's left hand.

Daisy smiled down at the ring. 'I don't think you've ever made anything more lovely, Rose. I don't know how you knew to make it but thank you.'

'It goes better with your wedding ring,' Rose said, but her eyes, so like Daisy's own, were sparkling with pride. 'You look beautiful, Daisy.'

'Will Seb recognise you without a hat?' Violet tucked an errant curl behind Daisy's ear and tweaked the flowers that held her twist of hair back into place. 'There, perfect.'

'You picked a good dress.' Rose was looking her up and down. 'Your boobs are a little bit bigger but otherwise you don't look pregnant.'

'I'm not showing yet!' Daisy still couldn't mention the pregnancy without blushing. She'd told her mother and sisters during her hen night while

Rose Skyped in; they had all been delighted. Especially as she hadn't needed to lie to them—they weren't just getting married because of the baby. They were getting married because they belonged together.

It was as simple and as wonderful as that.

Seb had expected to feel nervous. He was used to standing in front of large crowds, used to speaking in public. But when he taught or lectured he put on a persona. This was him, raw and exposed, in tails and a yellow cravat, ready to pledge his troth to the woman he loved.

He bit back a wry smile. He was even using her terminology now.

Sherry sat at the front, resplendent in something very structured and rigid. Seb knew very little about fashion but he was aware she was wearing something very expensive that mere mortals would never be able to carry off.

The buzz of voices came to a sudden stop as the band struck up one of Rick's most famous tunes, a song he had composed soon after Daisy's birth. The familiar chords sounded even more poignant than ever as a violin picked up the vocal lines, soaring up into the beams as one of the twins,

Seb had no idea which one, solemnly began to walk down the central aisle followed by the other.

And then his heart stopped as Daisy appeared. All in white except for her red lipstick and the bouquet of daisies, her eyes shining and a trembling smile on her lips. His fiancée, his bride, the mother of his baby.

Two months ago he was struggling on alone. Now he had a family, hope, joy. He had a future.

He smiled as a camera flashed from the back of the hall. Let them take photos, let them publish them everywhere and anywhere. He was the luckiest man alive and he was happy for the whole world to know.

* * * * *

MILLS & BOON®
Large Print – August 2015

THE BILLIONAIRE'S BRIDAL BARGAIN
Lynne Graham

AT THE BRAZILIAN'S COMMAND
Susan Stephens

CARRYING THE GREEK'S HEIR
Sharon Kendrick

THE SHEIKH'S PRINCESS BRIDE
Annie West

HIS DIAMOND OF CONVENIENCE
Maisey Yates

OLIVERO'S OUTRAGEOUS PROPOSAL
Kate Walker

THE ITALIAN'S DEAL FOR I DO
Jennifer Hayward

THE MILLIONAIRE AND THE MAID
Michelle Douglas

EXPECTING THE EARL'S BABY
Jessica Gilmore

BEST MAN FOR THE BRIDESMAID
Jennifer Faye

IT STARTED AT A WEDDING...
Kate Hardy

MILLS & BOON®
Large Print – September 2015

THE SHEIKH'S SECRET BABIES
Lynne Graham

THE SINS OF SEBASTIAN REY-DEFOE
Kim Lawrence

AT HER BOSS'S PLEASURE
Cathy Williams

CAPTIVE OF KADAR
Trish Morey

THE MARAKAIOS MARRIAGE
Kate Hewitt

CRAVING HER ENEMY'S TOUCH
Rachael Thomas

THE GREEK'S PREGNANT BRIDE
Michelle Smart

THE PREGNANCY SECRET
Cara Colter

A BRIDE FOR THE RUNAWAY GROOM
Scarlet Wilson

THE WEDDING PLANNER AND THE CEO
Alison Roberts

BOUND BY A BABY BUMP
Ellie Darkins

0815 Rom LP